SILVER

As told on *Jackanory*

BBC BOOKS

Published by BBC Books
a division of BBC Enterprises Limited,
Woodlands, 80 Wood Lane, London W12 0TT

First published 1991

ISBN 0 563 36171 9

Typeset in 13/16pt Garamond by Butler & Tanner Ltd, Frome
Printed and bound in England by Butler & Tanner Ltd, Frome

Contents

ARABEL'S TREE-HOUSE

by Joan Aiken

It had all started a month before, when a fierce gale blew down part of the Jones's garden wall, and ripped a big patch of tiles off the roof. The damaged roof could be fixed. Builders came and began slowly mending that. And Mortimer, the Jones family's raven, loved watching the men at work, specially after they installed a great yellow chute like a giant tube of macaroni, for dropping down broken tiles and rubble from the roof to ground level. It was Mortimer's chief hope that, somehow, one day, he would be able to get to the top of that tube and slide down it. So far, the builders had not allowed this.

But the garden wall could not be repaired so easily. First lawyers had to decide whether the wall belonged to the Joneses or to their neighbour Mr Leggit and, until that was agreed, and the hole mended, Mr Leggit's giant rabbit, Hoppy, was able to come through the gap into the Jones's garden whenever he liked.

Hoppy was about the size of a motor mower, without its grassbox, and he could do quite as much damage as a mower. Although at least ten years old, when he chose, he could be very active. Luckily he was rather slow-witted and lazy. Quite often, days went by when he forgot about the gap in the wall and merely pottered in his own garden. When he did come through, Arabel Jones worried all the time until he went back, because Mortimer the raven hated Hoppy with a fierce hate, and she was obliged either to keep Mortimer indoors, or to take him for long outings.

If Mortimer and Hoppy ever got into a fight, Arabel was not at all sure which would win, but she *was* sure they could do each other a lot of damage. Mortimer was quicker on his feet and had a deadly beak, but Hoppy was much bigger and heavier, and the terror of all the local cats. He would suddenly turn and kick them with his hind feet. As Mr Jones said, Hoppy could kick a golf ball through a bearskin hat. Not that anybody in the Jones family had a bearskin hat.

So, one morning, Arabel's heart sank when she looked through the kitchen window and noticed Hoppy just outside, slowly munching his way into a clump of pink asters. Mortimer had not seen Hoppy. He was eating a favourite breakfast of his, fish fingers spread with Gentleman's Relish and toasted. They were not his *very* favourite breakfast – which was sardines coated with salt meringue and baked in the oven – but that, said Mrs Jones, was too expensive and fiddly for weekdays. Mrs Jones was busy at present trying to clean up the dust and mess which the builders tracked through the house four times a day as they slowly mended the roof.

"And now poor old Aunt Elspeth has to go and die, and leave us the contents of her deep-freeze which I'm *sure* we don't want, whatever it is," she wailed, reading a letter that had just arrived on the mat. "Not that I blame the poor old lady for dying. She was ninety-four, after all, but you'd think there'd be some person a bit handier that she could leave the stuff in her freezer to, without having it sent all the way to London from Wales."

"At least we're getting the freezer as well," said Mr Jones, taking the letter and reading it, "though Lord knows where we can put a second freezer. Have to go in the wash-house, I reckon."

"All we need is another freezer cluttering up the wash-house! – not but what the one in the kitchen is stuffed to the

6

hinges with food that bird fancies for a week and then goes off: rotten apples and mouldy doughnuts. I don't know ..." And Mrs Jones stumped away to do the stairs with her Pixiette Mini-Cleaner. The trouble was that Mortimer preferred both apples and doughnuts when they had been kept a week or two and gone rather furry.

"Want to come with me in the cab this morning, Arabel, pet?" said Mr Jones. "I've a job fetching a package from Rumstead airport, so I could take you and the bird for a ride – so long as he behaves himself. That'd keep him and Hoppy from getting into a scrap."

"Oh, yes, Pa!" said Arabel joyfully. "Mortimer would like that, wouldn't you, Mortimer?"

"Kaaaark," said Mortimer, peering into the toaster to see if there were any fish fingers left inside, which there were not.

"I'll be glad when he's through *that* phase," said Mr Jones, putting on his jacket. "Don't fancy my toast and marmalade flavoured with haddock. Ready, both of you? Hurry up, Mortimer. I'm taking Arabel and the bird for an airing, Martha!" he bawled up the stairs.

"Mind you're back at twelve then. That's when the freezer's due," Mrs Jones called down. "And, Ben, while you're out, get some boards to repair Arabel's tree-house. And some wire netting."

"All right, all right," said Mr Jones. "Wire netting won't keep that rabbit out of our garden though. He'll be under it before you can say channel tunnel."

Arabel's tree-house had blown down in the gale along with the roof tiles, and she missed it a great deal. It had been a wooden platform, with rails, in the big pink double cherry at the bottom of the garden. In fine weather she and Mortimer spent a lot of time up there. Arabel carried Mortimer up in a basket (he hated flying) and, of course, Hoppy could not get up there.

Mr Jones drove to Rumstead airport where he discovered, to his annoyance, that they had a new ticket system for the car-park. You pulled a ticket from a machine when you entered, and you were supposed to put the ticket, and the right money, in another machine when you left.

"Why do they want all those machines?" said Mr Jones crossly. "It's humans what need jobs, not machines. I'll have to get some change before we leave. You'd best wait here in the taxi, Arabel dearie. I'll try not to be long. We've got to hurry home because of that perishing freezer."

Arabel and Mortimer didn't mind waiting in the multi-storey car-park. Mr Jones had left his taxi on an outside row of the first level, so she and Mortimer had a good view of the road below where there was a sign that said "Pick-Up Point". Mortimer liked watching the traffic flow along the one-way system, and the huge planes that suddenly floated overhead, coming down to land.

"NEVERMORE!" he said, each time, deeply impressed.

It was quite early, and there were still empty places in the car-park. Suddenly, after three or four planes had landed, the narrow street below became full of activity and commotion. First a group of skinny, long-legged black-haired men, wearing white caps and kilts like Scots, sprinted along and vanished into the car-park entrance. Next came two fleets of police cars, flashing lights and sounding sirens. They were going in opposite directions and narrowly avoided collisions with one another. Some of them did not avoid collisions.

"My goodness, Mortimer," said Arabel, "do you think someone has stolen a plane?"

"Kaaaark," said Mortimer.

One of the skinny kilted strangers had run up the spiral ramp and now came panting towards Arabel and Mortimer in their taxi.

"Is taxi free?" he said.

Arabel shook her head.

"Does person need ticket to take car from here?" he asked. His accent was very foreign.

"Yes," said Arabel.

At that he turned round, pounced on a business man who was just getting into his Rover, grabbed the white ticket from his hand, wrapped what looked like a piece of tartan blanket round the man's head and, with help from a skinny friend, stuffed the startled driver into the back of his own car. They jumped in and drove off at top speed down the ramp.

"Kaaaark!" said Mortimer, delighted.

Now Mr Jones arrived, very cross indeed as he had had a lot of trouble with the customs while getting the package (a box of rare orchids for a nursery gardener) and, after that, even worse trouble with the ticket machine, which swallowed his five pound note, and then lit a sign that said "YOU NEED ASSISTANCE".

"I don't need assistance, I need my fiver back," growled Mr Jones. "It *can't* cost five pounds – not yet, I should hope – for a half-hour in the airport car-park."

By the time this was sorted out, the two fleets of police cars had circled the entire airport complex and were ready to run into each other again outside the car-park entrance, just as Mr Jones came out.

"What is all this about?" he grumbled, as his taxi was halted by a road-block of police motorbikes and rubbish bins hastily thrown together.

"Hijackers!" shouted one policeman.

"Stowaways! One of them's a bear!" shouted another policeman.

"A *bear*? You've got to be kidding," said Mr Jones. "Anyway, all I have is a parcel of orchid roots, a raven and a girl who is my daughter Arabel."

The police were highly suspicious of Mortimer. "Did he come from overseas? How do you know he hasn't got rabies? Or Psittacosis?" they demanded. "Have you seen anyone behaving in a felonious way?"

"Certainly not," said Mr Jones. "Mortimer's an English raven. Born and bred in Rumbury Town. Now let me get on, please."

Arabel didn't know what felonious meant, so she kept quiet. Mortimer said, "Nevermore." At last the police let them through, and Mr Jones drove out of the airport by a back road

intended for supplies, as the front entrance was choked by
police vehicles rushing in all directions.

"Oh *look*, Pa!" said Arabel. "There's something that would
be just right for my tree-house. There, see! By the side of the
road. Someone must have thrown it away."

"Hmmmm," said Mr Jones, slowing as he approached it.

The thing was about the size of a double mattress, fawn-
coloured. It seemed to be made of many layers of softish,
crispish, stiffish material, all stuck together. It was very light.

"Well . . ." said Mr Jones, after some thought and looking
around him, "seeing as how no one else don't seem to want
it – I don't say but what it wouldn't be just the job."

And without more ado he hove it up on to the taxi roof and
strapped it to the rack with a bit of cord. Then they drove
home fast, for they were only just going to be in time to receive
Aunt Elspeth's freezer, even without stopping for wire netting.

The freezer, when man-handled with terrible difficulty into
the wash-house (it was very large and exceptionally heavy),
proved to be full to the brim with portions of Aunt Elspeth's
home-made carrot cake. Wrapped in foil, they were still frozen.

The portions were the size of bricks.

"When shall we *ever* eat it all?" wailed Mrs Jones. "*You* don't like it, Ben, and Mortimer went off it – unless it's mouldy – and Arabel comes out in spots if she eats too much. And *I'm* on Dr Parkinson's Short Sharp Slim-You-Up System."

"Well, we'll think of something," said Mr Jones. "Maybe you can have one of your Ladies' Coffee Mornings."

And he hoisted the fawn-coloured slab off the taxi roof and went to jam it into the crotch of the pink cherry tree, where it fitted precisely.

"I'll nail it and put a rail round this evening. Don't you climb on it till I've done that, Arabel dearie," he warned, and went to drive a duchess to open a public swimming pool in Kilburn. Luckily Hoppy was asleep in his hutch, full of asters, so Mortimer and Arabel were able to have their garden to themselves during the afternoon. Arabel draped a blanket over the hole in the wall.

At tea-time Mrs Jones was all excited.

"Such doings at Rumstead airport!" she said. "I heard on Radio 4. Some old-time dancers pinched a plane from Eastern Krk and flew it to England . . ."

"Where's Eastern Krk?" asked Arabel.

"I'm not sure, but they managed to land the plane at Rumstead and jumped out, and took *another* plane, and flew off somewhere else."

"Dancers?" said Arabel. "Then that's who those thin men in kilts were!"

Mrs Jones was not attending. She went on, "When the security men were looking over the stolen plane, what do you think they found? Stowaways just getting out of the baggage hold – imagine it! A man and his bear!"

"His bear?"

"A giant silver something! With six toes! And it's still At Large!" said Mrs Jones. "Fancy! It may be anywhere! The airport's only eight miles from here. You'd better stay indoors, Arabel, you and Mortimer both. That bird would be no match for a giant silver six-toed Bihorian bear."

"What about Hoppy?"

"Hoppy can look out for himself. He's not our worry."

Sure enough, on the six o'clock TV news, it was confirmed that the entire National Folk Dance Company of the small republic of Transylvanian Krk had escaped from their homeland in a stolen government aircraft, leaving the plane, which had run out of fuel, at Rumstead, and hijacking another, in which they were now on their way to Iceland, while two stowaways on the plane had emerged with their belongings and evaded the airport police for a while, but were now in custody after a fierce struggle.

One of them was a man, one a bear. The man gave his name as Eril Tahul, the bear was a giant silver six-toed Apusenian fruit-eating bear, once common all over the mountains of Europe, now very rare, and extremely ferocious (especially if female, as this one was). The man was in Rumbury jail, the bear in the zoo.

"Just fancy!" said Mrs Jones. "All that going on at the airport and you never knew."

"Just as well," said Mr Jones, flapping into his *Evening Spy.* He had fixed Arabel's tree-house.

Arabel felt sorry for the bear, shut in a foreign zoo and parted from her human friend.

"Maybe they don't even know what she likes to eat, Mortimer."

"Kaaaark," said Mortimer sadly.

A month later it was announced on the news that both captives had escaped. "Experts believe there must be some mysterious telepathic link between the man and the bear," said the newsreader, "for why else should they escape on the same day? Members of the public are warned not to approach them, as they may be highly dangerous, especially the bear. The man's real identity is still not known; the name he gave was false. Meanwhile there has been the first free election in Eastern Krk for fifty years. The government has been overthrown . . ."

That night, Arabel found it hard to sleep. She thought she heard a sorrowful voice calling through the streets of Rumbury Town: "Wodjina! Wodjina!"

Then she heard a small, sad noise which seemed to be in the garden. She slipped out of bed and tiptoed to the window. Mortimer was on the sill.

"Errrrch," he said softly.

"What's that out there, Mortimer? Is it a ghost?"

It looked very like a ghost. It was a huge, pale shape, forlorn, wandering about in the misty moonlight. Now and then it let out a whimpering moan.

"It wants something, Mortimer," said Arabel. "It sounds *dreadfully* sad. Do you think it's hungry?"

The builders' yellow waste-pipe still hung temptingly close to Arabel's window, with an even more tempting gash in it, which had been torn by a jagged piece of TV aerial. The pipe was not so very steep, after all.

"It would be just like going down a playground chute," said Arabel thoughtfully.

She put on a warm sweater and jeans over her nightie, opened the bottom of the window, and climbed into the hole in the big yellow tube. Then she let herself down by her hands.

"If you come too, Mortimer, you must keep QUIET," she whispered.

"Errrrch."

Then Arabel vanished down the pipe. Mortimer followed,

with a single, joyful stifled "Kaaaark!" as he shot into the dark.

When he caught up with Arabel, she was under the big cherry tree, talking very sympathetically to something large and pale and sad, about the size of a petrol pump, and stroking it.

"I feel dreadfully sorry for you – the only one left, and you don't know where Mr Tahul is. Are you hungry? I wonder what you like to eat?"

The white shape let out a mournful sound, "Arrrrgh ...!"

"Oh, my goodness! You must be starving, poor thing. I wonder if you would eat carrot cake? There's some in the wash-house."

The wash-house had a door leading to the garden, and a spare key lived under a brick in case any of the Jones family accidentally got locked out. Arabel fetched half a dozen portions of frozen carrot cake.

"Wait, wait – you have to take off the foil! Oh, you *do* like it! I *am* pleased! You don't mind its being frozen? Maybe you like it that way? Maybe things mostly *are* frozen in the Apusenian mountains?"

The newcomer was plainly ready to go on eating carrot cake for a long time. (Mortimer helped too, recalling that at one time he had been very keen on Aunt Elspeth's carrot cake, until she came to stay and made it every day for three weeks.)

At last the visitor gave a great yawn, turned, and climbed the ladder that led to the tree-house.

"Do you think that platform will bear your weight?" asked Arabel anxiously.

It did. It might have been made for the purpose. A snore came from above.

Next day Arabel said, "Ma, may I put my Indian tent in the tree-house?"

"All right, dearie," said Mrs Jones, who was planning a coffee morning next week to use up all that carrot cake, "only fetch it in if it rains. Now where did I put all those paper plates and serviettes left from Brenda's birthday?"

The garden was all misty with September mist. The visitor was still up in the cherry tree looking like the ghost of an iceberg.

"NEVERMORE!" said Mortimer, really impressed.

"I *think* she's called Wodjina," said Arabel, "but *I* think Wodge suits her better."

Hoppy the rabbit was squatting in the rockery. He was gaping with wonder – his two front teeth stuck out like prongs. He plainly thought the new arrival was the largest tree-climbing white rabbit in the world. He was quite subdued.

Arabel had brought a wheelbarrow-load of carrot cake, and she climbed with a couple of portions on to the platform.

"Oh, Mortimer," she breathed in astonishment, "there's a baby now as well!"

"Kaaaark?" said Mortimer cautiously.

The baby was unbelievably tiny, considering the hugeness of its mother. She was bigger than a church door. He was about the size of a dandelion puff.

"I won't touch him, Wodge," said Arabel soothingly to the nervous mother, "but isn't he beautiful! I'll put up this tent, so people won't notice you in the tree." Wodge and her puffball baby just fitted inside the tent.

"I wonder where poor Mr Tahul has got to?" said Arabel, "or whatever he's really called."

They found out Mr Tahul's name on the one o'clock news.

"The people of Eastern Krk have elected a new president," said the announcer, "replacing Mr Aram Tosh is the well known Krkan poet Bruno Kopychintzy, who has often been in prison for his liberal views. Recently he escaped from Krk with a bear, the last surviving specimen of the great silver Apusenian species, because he claimed the bear should have her cub in freedom, not under a tyrannical regime. Mr Kopychintzy is a keen environmentalist ..."

"Poor man, and they took and stuck him in Rumbury jail," said Mrs Jones. "I suppose he spoke only Krk and couldn't explain himself. I wonder where I put grandma's recipe for shrimp salad ...? Funny, I thought the builders had all gone, but there's one of them now, in the garden ..."

Arabel and Mortimer went out into the garden where Wodge and Mr Kopychintzy were hugging each other in a frenzy of joy.

"Cherkha harin ixan chipiena," he said to Arabel, who was bringing more carrot cake. And he kissed both her hands. "Oh, cherkha, cherkha!"

"I'm afraid there won't be quite enough room in the tent for both of you and the baby," said Arabel. "But I suppose you don't really need to stay there. Perhaps you haven't heard that you are president of Krk?"

"Oro?"

"You – are – president – of Krk."

"Oro?"

Luckily, at this moment Mr Jones arrived back from driving six children to dancing class.

"Who the blazes is that in your tree-house, Arabel?" he said. "And why are Hoppy and Mortimer playing ring-a-rosy round the cherry tree?"

"Because the baby's so beautiful! This gentleman is the president of Krk, Pa," said Arabel. "And I think you'd better find someone who speaks the Krk language, so we can tell him they want him back at home."

Mr Jones phoned the Krkan embassy, and Count Kpvaff the ambassador came and soon had everything sorted out. Mr

Bruno Kopychintzy, after some explanation, at last understood that he need not wander through the streets of Rumbury Town dodging the English police and calling for his lost bear. He and Wodjina were free to return, he to be president, she to live in the Apusenian mountains with her cub.

The birth-mat, which all silver six-toed Apusenian fruit-bears build from birch bark and acacia leaves, they decided to leave behind.

"They wish to present the birth-mat to you, Mr Jones, if you please," said Count Kpvaff, "as a thank-offering for your hospitality. They came here because the former Krkan government would put Wodjina in a zoo. This Mr Kopychintzy does not approve."

"I should think not!" said Arabel.

A procession of ten Rolls-Royces came to fetch the visitors away, and they were officially seen off at Rumstead airport by a Guards band playing the Krkan national anthem.

Hoppy and Mortimer had been so awestruck by the size of their visitor that they remained quite mild, even friendly, for several weeks until the wall was mended.

All remained calm in the Jones household until the day of Mrs Jones's coffee morning, when she looked into the freezer that had contained Aunt Elspeth's carrot cake . . .

LIZZIE DRIPPING BY MOONLIGHT

by Helen Cresswell

——————

Lizzie Dripping often felt a prickle at the back of her neck when she read a poem she liked. It was rather like the prickle she felt whenever she went tiptoe and breath-held into the graveyard to see if the witch was there – *her* witch. Not exactly the same, because with a poem it was a prickle of delight. With the witch it was fright and delight.

Although Lizzie thought of her as *her* witch, and a friend of sorts, she was a tricky customer. She came and went as she pleased, refused to tell her name and was quite capable of turning cats into toads.

> *Slowly, silently, now the moon*
> *Walks the night in her silver shoon;*
> *This way, and that, she peers, and sees*
> *Silver fruit upon silver trees.*

Lizzie, who up till now had been daydreaming, as usual, felt that delicious, slow tingle along her spine. Her teacher was a good reader, and she picked good poems. Lizzie listened spellbound and the tingle was still there when the poem ended.

> *A harvest mouse goes scampering by,*
> *With silver claws and silver eye;*
> *And moveless fish in the water gleam,*
> *By silver reeds in a silver stream.*

Miss Platt's voice stopped. Lizzie waited. Surely there was more? She wanted the poem to go on and on.

19

"Is that all?" she asked. The rest of the class tittered and Lizzie felt her face fire.

"I'm afraid so," said Miss Platt. "Though you could always try writing another verse of your own." So she could, thought Lizzie Dripping. And she might, at that. But what she already longed for was to see a silver world of her own.

Was it *really* silver, at night, under the moon? Did trees, hedges, field and farm gleam and shine as if brushed with frost? Would the cows have silver eyes, and the sheep? Best of all, would she *herself* be silver?

At dinner time she asked Patty, her mother.

"Mam, does the world really go silver at night?"

"What?" Patty was dishing out the shepherd's pie, and only half listening, as usual. "Does the what?"

"World go silver. At night. When there's a moon, I mean."

"That's just your daft kind of question, Lizzie Dripping," her mother told her.

"Bit difficult to tell, these days," said Albert, her father. "It's the street lights, see. Neither moon nor stars, when there's street lights. But in the old days ... aye ... I reckon it *was* kind of silvery."

"Then you've different eyes from *mine*," Patty told him. "Silver!"

And just then Toby set up yelling, and that was the end of that. It was the end of the conversation, at any rate. But Lizzie Dripping went on thinking, and what she wondered now was whether the moon was full.

That night, after Patty had gone back downstairs, Lizzie climbed out of bed and drew back the curtain. She could see the dark shape of the church tower and the sheep under the apple trees in the field opposite. The street lamps were orangey when you looked at them, but they didn't give a golden light. Lizzie's gaze travelled upwards and – her breath caught in her

throat – the moon! It was there, full and round and white, hanging above the roof of Bell Brigg farm. Lizzie's spine dissolved into a long, slow tingle.

"Tomorrow," she thought. "Tomorrow night!" Because Lizzie Dripping had already decided that if there *were* a silver world out there, she was going to discover it. "I'd have to go out the village," she thought, as she lay plotting her plot. "In the fields, where there's no light." The thought was a little frightening, though she didn't see why.

"There'll only be sheep and cows," she thought, "and mice and that, with silver claws and silver eye." Then, "The witch!"

That was a very different kettle of fish. If Lizzie was to go walking out of Little Hemlock alone, at night, then the last thing she wanted to know was that the witch was about. A witch in broad daylight and only a stone's throw away from home was one thing. A witch at night, by moonlight, was definitely another. There was only one thing to do.

Next day was Saturday. Lizzie, as usual, was sent up to the shop, and as usual was told to give Toby a push.

"Does he *have* to go?"

Lizzie was going to call at the graveyard, as well as the shop. "I think he's bored with being pushed up to the shop."

"Of course he ain't, are you, my lamb?" Patty lifted Toby and plonked him in his pushchair.

"You're a nuisance," Lizzie told him as she pushed him down the path. "Toby Arbuckle's a great fat nuisance, Toby Arbuckle's a great fat nuisance!" Toby gurgled plumply and waved his knitted cat by the tail.

"Well, don't blame *me* if you get turned toad!" Lizzie told him. A while back, she had seen with her own eyes the Briggs' black and white tom turned into a toad. Luckily, the witch had been in a good mood that day, and had turned him back again.

"If that witch turns *Toby* into a toad, I'll never be able to go back home again," thought Lizzie Dripping. "Not ever."

Up at the shop she bought the things for her mother and then spent part of her pocket money on sweets for Toby. "To keep him quiet," she thought. "Then I'll push him into the church porch, where the witch can't see him."

Though she could not be sure, not absolutely sure, that the witch *wouldn't* see him. For all she knew, that witch could see through stone. She reached the church and pushed Toby by the steep, grassy bank that she always thought of as a pathway into the sky. When she reached the little wrought iron gate at the top she stopped and listened. Only the whistle of birds, the soft sough of wind in the seeding grasses, the bleat of lambs from the home field. Lizzie took a deep breath and went through the gate. She wheeled Toby into the porch, then gave him the sweets.

"You stop here, Toby," she told him. "Lizzie'll be back soon." As she turned the corner of the church her eyes went straight to the wide flat tomb of "Hannah Post of this parish" and "Albert Cyril, beloved husband of the above 1802–1879. Peace, Perfect Peace." That was where the witch would sit, endlessly knitting in black wool what looked like a shawl for a witch baby. Not there!

Lizzie was not surprised. The witch could make herself visible or invisible in the blink of any eye. And she liked playing hide-and-seek. Lizzie called softly.

"Witch? Witch, where are you?" No reply. Not even the twitch of a grass by the tomb of the Perfectly Peaceful Posts. "It's me! Lizzie!" Silence. Then – Lizzie stiffened – a thin, high cackle from somewhere near, somewhere behind her. Round she whirled. Nothing. Not a sign.

"Knit one, purl one, slip one, knit one, pass the slip stitch over . . ."

Slowly, breath held, Lizzie turned again. There she sat, her witch, hunched over her tattered knitting. "I spy with my little eye!" The witch did not even look up.

"Oh witch! You *are* there!" Lizzie edged closer, but not too close. "It looks smashing. Your knitting, I mean."

"S'all right," said the witch. "What d'you want?"

"Oh! Oh, nothing," Lizzie lied. "Just wanted to see you, that's all."

The witch did look at her now, with her fierce bright eyes. It was as if she could see right through Lizzie – read her thoughts, even. Lizzie swallowed hard.

"Witch . . ."

"Well? What is it, girl?"

"I wondered . . . I mean, when I come to see you, it's always daytime, see. What I wondered . . . is . . . do you come at night, as well?"

"Day, night, sun, moon – 's'all the same to me!" The witch's black mittened hands were working her needles again.

"So – you do come out at night?"

"Maybe do – maybe don't!" said the witch unhelpfully. Click click went the wooden needles. Lizzie decided to try another tack.

"Witch – there's a full moon. When there is ... is ... does the world turn silver?" The witch stuck her pins into the ball of wool and thrust her knitting deep into the black folds of her cloak. She sat then, musing, rocking a little from side to side. And when she did speak, it was in a dreamy, singsong way, as if to herself. "Moonlight ... owl light ... bat light ..." she crooned, "*witch* light ..."

"Oh dear," thought poor Lizzie Dripping. "She *does* come out at night."

"Bats fly, owls hoot, witches ride ... and the moon's huge and white, and the whole world's ..." she paused.

"Yes?" prompted Lizzie softly, hardly daring, "Yes?"

"Silver ..." The witch whispered the word, stroked it, as if it were a cat. "Silver!"

"Ah ..." Lizzie let out a long held breath. So the witch did inhabit the world of the night and the witch saw a world of silver at every full moon. "Oh," she said, and now she too was speaking her thoughts aloud. "Oh, I'd give anything to see it, anything!"

"Then see it, girl, see it!" the witch snapped. She was back

to her usual self again now, tart and crabby.

"But I can't! I mean . . . I mean . . ."

"Daren't?" suggested the witch slyly, tilting her head. "Daren't – because of me?"

"Yes. No . . . oh, I don't know!" Lizzie was almost in tears now.

"But *I* know." The witch looked at her now, very long and hard. "*I* know . . ." And as she spoke, she vanished. She did not vanish in a twinkling, as she usually did. She faded, dissolved into the green air by the hedge. Lizzie strained into the shadows, but there was not the least hint that the witch might still be there, even invisibly there.

"Witch?" she called. "Witch?" She wheeled about, scanning the leaning, barnacled tombstones, the knee-high grass and wind-bent trees. The world was suddenly empty and bleak, as it always was after the witch vanished.

"But she's there somewhere," Lizzie comforted herself. "Must be. Invisibly there."

Then she remembered Toby, and found him smothered in chocolate in the church porch. He beamed, a sticky beam.

"Look at you! Just look at you!" The smile faded. The round blue eyes fixed anxiously on Lizzie's. In a flash she was contrite. She had spoilt his morning just as the witch had spoilt hers.

"Oh Toby! 'S'not your fault! Come on, sausage – Lizzie loves you!" And she swept him up from his chair, chocolate and all, and hugged him. And even as she did so she knew that it was as much to comfort herself as him.

The rest of the day, the long stretch that lay between sun and moonlight, was long and unsatisfactory. Lizzie loved Saturdays, as a rule. She dawdled and dreamed her way through them as sleek and happy as a cat – if Patty let her. Today, she could settle to nothing. The world itself seemed drained of colour, drab and dull. Lizzie's thoughts were fixed on another world entirely – a silver one. She felt that she would die if she couldn't see it. To relieve her feelings, she *did* write another verse to the poem Miss Platt had read:

> *I walk the night down the quiet lane*
> *White and shining as if with rain,*
> *Down to the fields where lie in peace*
> *Silvery sheep with their silver fleece.*

She was quite pleased with it, in a way. "Only thing is, it's a cheat," she thought. "I haven't been down the lane at night, nor seen silvery sheep." What was worse, she couldn't be sure that she ever would. For all she knew, she had that witch for life. And now she knew for a fact that the witch came out at night.

She would be there, lurking in the spiky shadows, brimming with spells. And Lizzie Dripping felt in her bones that night spells were dangerous, not to be sneezed at.

"Dare I?" she wondered. "Or daren't I?" She never gave a

thought to Patty, and what she would say if she found that Lizzie was up and out by night, walking the fields alone in the moonlight.

"Easy enough to slip out," she thought. "They'll be watching the telly and never notice." Even if, by some stroke of ill luck, Patty did find out, it was not the end of the world. But if, out there in the wide, moon-bleached fields, she met a witch – that might be the end of the world.

It went on all day. "Dare I ... daren't I? Dare I ... daren't I?" In the end, she didn't have to decide. It was at teatime when the blow fell. "Lucky Blod was free," Lizzie heard her mother say, "else we couldn't've gone."

"Gone where?" demanded Lizzie.

"Whist Drive, tonight, at the village hall. Your Aunt Blodwen's coming to babysit."

"Oh no!" It was one thing to get past Patty and Albert, another thing entirely to get past Aunt Blod, with her sharp Welsh eyes and sharp Welsh ears. Lizzie's beautiful world of

silver splintered like glass before her eyes. "Now I'll never see it," she thought. "Never. Not till the next full moon, anyhow." But the next full moon was light years away, an eternity. "I'll die," thought Lizzie Dripping. "I'll just die." She told herself this quite often.

At just before seven Aunt Blod arrived with her knitting, and Albert and Patty went off.

"Bed at eight, mind, Lizzie," Patty called as she went.

"I'll see to it, Patty," Blod said. "Don't believe in children up all hours, watching telly and ruining their eyes." The back door shut.

"I don't watch telly," Lizzie told her coldly. "I read."

"Ruin your eyes just as easy reading," said Aunt Blod smugly. "Eight o'clock, Lizzie, and not a moment after." In the end, Lizzie went to bed early. Better to lie in bed reading than stop with Aunt Blod and the click click click of her needles.

"Nearly dark!" Lizzie peered through the curtains. The moon was already hanging there, but pale and washed out. The street lamps glowed orange and she could see the lights of the village hall by the church.

"If ever I'm prime minister," she told herself savagely, "there'll be a law against street lamps!" She dropped the curtain and climbed into bed. She had a good book – one about a boy who was snatched away by an eagle – but she could not keep her mind on it. All the time, mixed in with pictures of the soaring eagle, were other pictures of a world in the moonlight, a silver world.

After about an hour she gave a sigh and looked at the clock on her bedside table. Nearly nine o'clock. "Dark outside, now," she thought. "At least, dark except for the moonlight. Just finish this chapter and – oh!"

The light went out. At the very same moment the music

and laughter from below, where Aunt Blod was watching television, stopped dead. For a moment there was darkness and silence. Then a shriek from Aunt Blodwen.

"Electricity cut," thought Lizzie. They had them, from time to time, and Patty always had candles ready. She could hear Aunt Blod stumbling about below, looking for them. Lizzie lay there, and as she did so became aware that the room was no longer dark. Her eyes went to the curtains – the pattern was showing, as it did first thing in the morning.

"The moon!" Lizzie was out of bed and at the window and then staring out at a new world. She had known the scene all her life, but now it lay foreign, strangely other under a broad, white light. The street lamp had been snuffed out like a candle and the moon had come into its own. Each apple tree in the orchard below was dappled silver and stood anchored in a sharp black shadow. The grass was bleached as if thick with hoar frost. Here and there lay the sheep. "Silvery sheep with their silver fleece! 'S'true, then! The world *does* turn silver!"

Down below Aunt Blodwen was muttering to herself, still searching for candles. Lizzie did not even hear her. She was gazing out at a world that till now she had hardly dreamed of, and thinking what a miracle it was that all the lights should go out tonight, of all nights. A miracle, or – the witch!

Was she out there, stalking the silver night, rubbing her skinny palms with glee. Could a witch make the lights go out?

Lizzie Dripping leaned right out of the open window and the moon shone full on her face and she could have sworn that she actually felt herself turn silver.

"Witch?" she called softly. "Witch! Thank you, witch!"

An owl hooted mournfully from the beeches down below. There was a sudden screech – which might have been that of a moorhen by the lake, frightened by a fox. Or might have been that of a witch ... a silver witch?

SILVER SEYMOUR, THE MILLIONTH MOGGY

by Joan Eadington

Emmy Lee was having a really good day at school. No one had told her off. No one had tried to grab anything off her, and the weather was brilliant.

And, to add to this perfection, Miss Clegg, their teacher, had just walked into the classroom with a fairly large box with air holes in it.

It could only mean one thing: a living, breathing mysterious creature.

The last mysterious creature had happened last week, when the headmaster of Seymour Drive Junior School found a guinea pig scuttling up and down the carpet in his office. So he put it in a box with air holes and wrote "Lost Property" on it in large letters. Then he advertised it in the school hall. It was claimed within three minutes.

But this box was bigger, and seemed heavy. And Miss Clegg was carrying it very carefully – as if there might be an explosion any minute.

The class was like a flock of goggle-eyed, long necked flamingoes leaning towards it, and the air was simmering with excitement as words like "man-eating spiders in bunches of bananas", "killer plants from outer space", and "the first vampire ever to be captured in the classroom cupboard", flashed about like fork lightning.

"It's something very common, and very scruffy," said Miss Clegg. "And it has silvery grey stripes and a white chest."

Then she told them this awful tale about how it had been found in the school yard by Mr Cork, the caretaker, in the school holidays, with its leg in the grips of a heavy gin trap. And how Mr Cork nursed "this 'ere Seymour," — from Seymour School yard — back to health, but couldn't find its rightful owner. And he couldn't keep "this Seymour pest" any longer, as it was the millionth Seymour moggy he'd rescued from the school yard in fifteen years.

"He's still hoping someone will be brave enough to admit it's theirs, or adopt it," said Miss Clegg. "And Mr Trent is going to put that huge, rusty gin trap with its sharp metal teeth on display in our 'Less Cruelty to Animals' day next week."

"Do they know who trapped it, Miss?" asked Gordon Shell, with anxious excitement, as half the class discussed exactly what the traps were used for, and found they were for trapping all sorts of animals, but were now illegal.

Then Miss Clegg asked them what "illegal" meant, and Donny Dobbs said it was something to do with not making your own whisky. But everyone else said it meant it was against the law and not allowed.

And all the time this interesting argy-bargy was going on, the other half of the class were whispering "Open the box. Open the box. We want to see the millionth moggy." And, in another second, there was this enormous, mournful "Meeiouooowwooooow."

"It needs a good, kind home," said Miss Clegg, lifting the box lid very, very gently. "It's had a hard life, and it needs to spend its last few years in peace and contentment."

A murmur of sympathy rippled round the class. But suddenly it turned to a huge gasp, as they saw this large striped, silvery, tiger-like head appear, and saw two wide glowing green eyes. And then – as the gasps grew louder – Silver Seymour sprang from the box with a growling hiss, just at the very moment when their classroom door opened and Richard Elms walked in, carrying an important message about the school window cleaners arriving.

Then, they all saw a solid, fat and furry mass whisk past Richard's bony legs, and it was obvious to all that Mr Cork the caretaker had nursed this millionth moggy back to bouncing health, because it shot out of the school and through the bent school railings, with everyone watching it from the windows.

"That's quite enough heart-attack excitement for one afternoon," sighed Miss Clegg. Then she said, "Ah well. At least it's solved our problem of finding it a permanent home. Sometimes a cat with a mystery history isn't always the best sort to settle down on silk cushions. Though the thought of yet another stray cat sadly wandering the streets isn't very cheerful."

On the way home from school that day, Emmy said to her friend Gordon, "I wish it had stayed. I'd love a cat like Silver Seymour. We haven't any pets in our house except human ones. My sister Emerald is Mam and Dad's pet. She never gets shouted at, even when she tips a bowl of cereal over her head and yowls all the time from her high chair. And my big brother Toby's pet is his girlfriend Marguerite. He calls her Margy-Pargy Turtle Dove and she calls him Toby-Doby Cuddly Panda."

Emmy and Gordon looked at each other knowingly, and shook their heads glumly. They were both wearing cotton T-shirts chosen from the clothes basket in the Save the Children shop. Emmy's was green stripes, and it suited her brown skin and frizzy hair. And Gordon's was bright orange, and matched his freckles and ginger fringe.

Then Gordon said, "My Mam says animals cost too much to feed and take a lot of looking after. I did once have a stick insect in a glass jar until the twig it was on got used for poking holes in the garden when Grandad used it as a dibber to plant seeds."

"Mmmm . . ." said Emmy. "Well at least two good things have happened. Silver Seymour was well enough to escape, and our school can at least show that terrible trap to the whole world on our 'Less Cruelty to Animals' day. But, oh, how I wish beautiful Silver Seymour would magic himelf to *my* house."

"And *I* wish we knew who left that trap lying about," said

33

Gordon, "so as to make people care more about not doing cruel things. Maybe someone had it to catch rabbits or something in the woods near school, and Silver Seymour was trapped instead and managed to drag himself to our school yard for help. Unless he was just dumped."

"Just imagine if you, or even me had got our foot trapped in it," whispered Emmy, shivering slightly.

All the way home from school that day, Emmy thought about poor old Silver Seymour.

But when she went into the back garden she could hardly believe her eyes! He was there, sitting on a log, blinking in the warm sunshine!

Was it really him? Lots of cats look alike.

Then she knew for certain, because he suddenly stood up and stretched, and she saw that one of his legs was bent and thin from the trap.

She went towards him happily, but in a second his mood changed. His hair stood on end and he began to hiss and growl. He looked ready to spring at her if she went an inch nearer. Then he shot away to a corner of the garden and stayed there, hissing like a tormented wild animal.

It was a real shock. He seemed to *hate* her. Emmy's heart sank.

Then she thought, "Perhaps if I gave him something to eat?" But what?

She went to where Mam kept food tins. And amongst all the soup and spaghetti and beans, she spotted two small tins of salmon. Cats like fish. She hesitated.

At least there were two tins. And their family never seemed to eat two tins at once. Mam usually made what she called salmon mousse, or mixed it with something else for sandwiches. So if Emmy just gave Seymour one small tin, which didn't seem much for a fairly big tom-cat, she could always use next week's pocket money in advance to buy Mam another one. It would mean next week's pocket money would be down to five pence, but it would be worth it.

She opened the tin with the wall can-opener, and was careful not to spill any of the juice because anyone could smell tinned fish a mile off. Then she tipped the salmon into a cereal dish. It looked bright orangey-pink and ever so tempting. But oh, how small for a wild cat as big as Silver Seymour who didn't know where his next meal was coming from.

Well, of course, Emmy's *real* plan was to carry the dish of salmon carefully into the garden and put it where Seymour could come and find it. Then perhaps he'd get a bit tamer.

But the next second Mam had come in with Emerald, Emmy's baby sister, from the nursery! "What on earth are you doing with that salmon?" She looked like thunder.

And before Emmy could even answer she said, "Don't imagine we're having it for our tea because I need both tins to make salmon sandwiches to take to Muriel's garden supper tonight in aid of the Darts Club outing."

Then Mam told Emmy to come in the other room and keep her eye on Emerald whilst Mam went upstairs.

Then, something awful happened.

Have you ever lived in a house where when you open the back door or the front door and another door is open, the wind blows right through and slams the other door?

Well, it was suddenly a bit windy. And with Mam just

coming in at the front, *that* door was open. And with Emmy coming in from the back garden, *that* door was open. But not for long. The back door suddenly slammed. The house shook and Emmy heard this terrible crash! And when she rushed into the kitchen the salmon was lying in a broken dish on the floor and crouching near the cupboard was a hissing, silver-streaked trapped robber tom-cat, looking ready to spring at her at any minute.

Emmy was terrified. It was like being in a lion's cage. But as quick as lightning she opened the back door again and in seconds Silver Seymour had rushed outside like a tornado.

"What on earth's happening?" shrieked Mam, grabbing hold of baby Emerald and looking at the salmon all over the floor.

With a sinking heart, Emmy tried to explain to Mam, but Mam wasn't in the least sympathetic. She just groaned and flopped in a chair whilst the kettle boiled for a cup of tea. "Trouble, trouble, trouble," she said. Then she relented a bit and said, "I know you were trying to be kind to a stray animal, but once you start feeding them they never leave you. And we don't want that, do we?"

Emmy's eyes prickled with tears as she thought of Silver Seymour's awful life. How dreadful for him to be frightened of all human beings and never to trust them.

After tea Mam said, "It's not the end of the world, Emmy. I've changed the sandwiches to cheese for the garden supper. Toby'll be here to keep an eye on things whilst Dad and I are out."

Emmy went into the garden and stood there sadly. Then she saw something silvery, not in their garden, but in Mrs Kelly's next door. It was Silver Seymour! And like a suction pump he was drinking a huge saucer of milk, with Mrs Kelly standing smiling.

"It's my sister's lost cat," she said to Emmy. "I'd know that silver streak anywhere. He lives just near your school. He's remembered me, he's purring."

Then, another surprise happened, because Gordon came round and they both told Mrs Kelly about the gin trap.

"I've found out about it," said Gordon. "I just met Donny Dobbs at the shops, and his brother's cousin's friend found one in a junk yard, but his parents made him get rid of it immediately, and he threw it in the woods last Christmas."

"He always was a mucky little litter-lout," said Emmy. "What a cruel, thoughtless thing to do."

They all stared at Silver Seymour, and he stared back. Then, slowly, he stretched himself and with one, quick spring disappeared over the fence.

"He'll be back," laughed Mrs Kelly, as Emmy told her and Gordon about the salmon.

That night, just before Emmy got into bed, she looked out at the clear night sky. It was pin-pointed with stars, and the moon was as thin as the silver scoop of a ladle. Then in the gleam of light from a window, she suddenly saw a familiar shape, sitting there peacefully, and she gave a sigh of happiness.

Oh yes, he'd be back. A million times . . .

A NARROW SQUEAK

by Dick King-Smith

―――――

"Do you realise," said Ethel, "that tomorrow is our Silver Wedding Day?"

"So soon?" said Hedley in a surprised voice. "How time flies! Why, it seems but yesterday that we were married."

"Well, it isn't," said Ethel sharply. "You only have to look at me to see that."

Hedley looked at her. "She seems to have put on a great deal of weight," he thought. "Not that she isn't still by far the most beautiful mouse in the world, of course, but there's a lot more of her now."

"You have certainly grown," he said tactfully.

"Grown?" snapped Ethel. "And whose fault is that, pray? Anyone would think you did not know why I am blown out like a balloon. Goodness knows what sort of a father you will make."

"A father?" said Hedley. "You mean . . .?"

"Any time now," said Ethel. "And I'm starving hungry, Hedley. Fetch us something nice to eat, do. I could just fancy something savoury."

She sighed deeply as her husband hurried away. "Was there ever such a mouse," she said to herself. "So handsome, but so thick. Let's hope he doesn't walk straight down the cat's throat. I wouldn't put it past him, and then there won't be any Silver Wedding."

A mouse's life is, of course, a short one, fraught with hazards. For those that survive their infancy, death looms in many shapes and forms, among them the cat, the poison bait and the trap, and mice have learned to commemorate

anniversaries in good time. "Better early than never" is a favourite mouse proverb, and Ethel and Hedley's Silver Wedding was to be celebrated twenty-five days after their marriage.

If they were lucky, they would go on to a Pearl, a Ruby, a Golden and, should they be spared to enjoy roughly two months of wedded bliss, to a Diamond Wedding Anniversary. Beyond that, no sensible mouse cared to think.

"If only Hedley was more sensible," Ethel thought as she lay, uncomfortably on account of the pressure within her, in her nest. "Not that he isn't still by far the most beautiful mouse in the world, of course, but he's so accident prone." Hardly a day passed when Ethel did not hear, somewhere about the house, a thin cry of alarm, indicating that Hedley had just had a narrow squeak.

"He goes about in a dream," she said to herself. "He doesn't *think*. Surely other mice do not stand in the path of vacuum cleaners, or absent-mindedly explore the interior of tumble-dryers, or come close to drowning in a bowl of cat's milk?"

In fact, Hedley was thinking quite hard as he emerged from the hole in the skirting-board that was the entrance to their home, and prepared to make his way across the kitchen floor.

"A father!" he murmured happily to himself. "I am to be a father! And soon! How many children will there be, I wonder? How many will be boys, how many girls? And what shall we call them? What fun it will be, choosing the names!"

This was what Ethel had meant when she said that Hedley did not think. Her thoughts were severely practical and filled with common sense, and she was quick to make up her mind. By contrast Hedley was a daydreamer and much inclined to be wool-gathering when, as now, he was following up an idea. He had just decided to call his eldest son Granville after a favourite uncle, when he bumped into something soft and furry, something that smelt, now that he came to think of it, distinctly unpleasant.

The cat, fast asleep in front of the Aga cooker, did not wake, but it twitched its tail. With a shrill cry Hedley ran for cover. The larder door was ajar, and he slipped in and hid behind a packet of Corn Flakes.

The noise he had made reached Ethel's ears, and filled her mind, as so often over the previous twenty-four days, with thoughts of widowhood. It also woke the cat, who rose, stretched and padded towards the larder.

"Not in there, puss!" said its owner, coming into her kitchen, and she shut the larder door. Hedley was a prisoner.

For some time he crouched motionless. As happened after such frights, his mind was a blank. But gradually his thoughts returned to those unborn children. The eldest girl, now – what was she to be called?

After a while Hedley decided upon Dulcibel, his grandmother's name. But then suppose Ethel did not agree? Thinking of Ethel reminded him of her last words.

"Fetch us something nice to eat, do," she had said. "I could just fancy something savoury."

Hedley raised his snout and sniffed. This little room, in which he had never been before, certainly smelled of all kinds of food, and this reminded him that he himself was a bit peckish. He began to explore the larder, climbing up on to its shelves and running about to see what he could find.

"I will have a snack," he said to himself, "to keep me going, and then I will find something really nice to take back to Ethel."

Much of the food in the larder was in cans or packets, but Hedley found a slab of fruit cake and some butter in a dish and a plate of cold chips. At last, feeling full, he hid behind a row of tins and settled down for a nap.

Meanwhile, back at the nest, Ethel was growing increasingly uneasy. "He must have had his chips," she thought, "and our children will be born fatherless." She was hungry, she was uncomfortable, and she was more and more worried that Hedley had not returned.

"Oh Hedley, how I shall miss you!" she breathed. "So handsome, but so thick."

While Hedley was sleeping off his huge meal, the larder door was opened.

"Just look at this cake!" a woman's voice said. "And these

leftover chips! And the butter – little footmarks all over it! We've got mice."

"Put the cat in there," said a man's voice.

"Can't do that or it'll be helping itself too."

"Well, set a trap then. And put some poison down."

Hedley slept the whole night through. He dreamed of happy times to come. In his dream, his handsome sons and his beautiful daughters had grown old enough to leave the nest, and he was taking them on a conducted tour of the house. Then boldly he led them all, Granville and Dulcibel and the rest, and their mother too, through the cat-flap and out into the garden; "For we will picnic," he said to them, "in the strawberry bed. The fruit is ripe and the weather exceedingly pleasant."

"Oh papa!" the children cried.

"What fun that will be!"

"But are you not afraid of the cat, Hedley dear?" said Ethel nervously.

"Ethel, Ethel," said Hedley. "When have you ever known me afraid of anything?" and the children chorused, "Oh brave papa!"

He woke from his dream with a number of other possible names for the impending family in mind – Eugene, Tallulah, Hereward and Morwenna were four that he particularly fancied – when he suddenly remembered with a sharp pang of guilt that Ethel was still unfed.

"I shall get the rough edge of her tongue," he thought, and he looked about for a tasty item of food, small enough for him to carry. He climbed down to a lower shelf and found something which had not, he was sure, been there before. It was a saucer containing a number of little blue pellets, and beside it there was an opened packet. Had Hedley been able to read, he would have seen that on the packet was written: MOUSE POISON. KEEP AWAY FROM DOMESTIC ANIMALS.

As it was, thinking how unusual and attractive the blue pellets looked, he took a mouthful of them. "She'll love these," he thought. "Such a pretty colour," and he ran down to the floor of the larder only to find the door shut.

"Bother," thought Hedley. "How am I to get out of this place?" He was considering this problem in a half-hearted way, for part of his mind was still occupied with names – would Annabel be better than Morwenna? – when his nose caught a most exciting smell. It was cheese, a little square lump of it, conveniently placed on the floor. The cheese was, in fact, on a little wooden platform, an odd-looking thing that had a metal arm and a spring attached to it. But Hedley, busy deciding that after all he preferred Morwenna, did not stop to think about this. "It's her favourite food," he said to himself, "and just the right size for me to carry back," and he spat out the little blue pellets and ran to grab the cheese. Whether it was his speed or whether the trap had not been lightly enough set, Hedley got away with it.

"Snap!" went the trap, missing him (though not by a whisker for it cut off three of them), and Hedley gave, through his mouthful of cheese, a muffled squeak of fright.

"Listen!" said the woman's voice, and "You got him!" said the man's, and the larder door was opened.

For once Hedley did not daydream. He streaked across the

kitchen floor and into his hole, the lump of cheese clenched in his jaws. Ethel regarded him silently from the nest.

"Sorry I'm late," he panted. "I got held up. Here, it's Farmhouse Cheddar, your favourite. How have you been?"

"Busy," said Ethel shortly.

"Busy?" said Hedley.

"Yes," said Ethel.

She attacked the cheese hungrily, while Hedley lay and got his breath back. "Funny," he thought, "she looks slimmer than yesterday. As slim, in fact, as the day we met, and what a meeting that was! I remember it as if it was yesterday.

"We literally ran into one another, in a narrow runway under the sitting-room floorboards, I recall, bumped noses in fact, for I remember how deliciously damp and cold Ethel's nose was.

" 'Frightfully sorry!' I said, and she replied, 'Why don't you look where you're going?' Yes, those were her very first words to me. 'I don't know,' I replied, for that was all I could think of to say, so taken aback was I. And then Ethel said, 'You don't look to me as if you even knew your own name.' And I said, 'Oh yes, I do. My name is ...'"

"Hedley!" said Ethel now, licking her lips as she finished the cheese. "You do know what day it is, don't you?"

"Wednesday, I think," said Hedley. "Or it may be Thursday. I am not sure."

"Hedley," said Ethel. "It is our Silver Wedding Day."

"Oh!" cried Hedley. "I quite forgot."

"Typical," thought Ethel. "He'd forget his head if it wasn't screwed on."

"I have a present for you," she said, and she rose and stood aside from the nest.

In the middle of a comfortable warm bed, composed of flock from a chair lining, and feathers from an eiderdown and a mass of scraps of newspaper, lay six fat pink naked babies.

"Three boys and three girls," she said. "Neat, eh?"

"Oh!" thought Hedley. "What could be neater! Granville and Dulcibel, Eugene and Tallulah, and Hereward and Morwenna."

"Oh Ethel dearest," he said. "I have no present for you but my love."

At these words Ethel's annoyance melted away. "What a fine looking mouse he still is," she thought, "not a grey hair on him. In fact he looks no older than he did at our wedding, twenty-five long days ago."

Hedley sat in a brown study, gazing at the babies. Then he said, "Oh Ethel! To think that you did this all on your own! You're so *clever*!"

"And you're so *thick*," thought Ethel fondly, but out loud she said, "Oh Hedley! You are *so* handsome!"

WHAT'S IT WORTH, JOEY?

by Robert Leeson

Just below the flats where Joey lived stood a row of small houses with tiny backyards and front doors that opened on to the pavement. The houses were old and grey and the people who lived in them were old, too. Oldest of all, so Joey thought, was Mr Hardacre, who kept the shop right at the end of the row.

The shop was small and its window was full of old clocks, brass candlesticks, ornaments, rings and buckles, jumbled together and covered in dust. Across the top of the window was written in faded letters: "Gold and silver bought. Highest prices paid."

Mr Hardacre must be very rich, if he could afford to buy gold and silver. But he didn't look rich. He was tall, thin and white haired. He wore a black suit, shiny with age, and a shirt open at the collar, without a tie. Over one eye he wore a patch, but the other eye was very blue and sharp, peering out under his bushy eyebrow.

Joey liked to stop and look at the strange collection in the window. But when Mr Hardacre stood in the doorway, glaring with that one fierce eye, Joey hurried past. He never dared go in.

Until one day.

Word went round the flats that the little street was coming down. The demolition men were coming with their great ball and chain, their picks and shovels. The walls would be smashed and clouds of dust would fly up in the air.

Already some of the old folk had begun to move out, taking their bits and pieces with them. Some of the houses were empty. The paint peeled off the front doors and one or two of the windows were broken.

Pogger and the gang from the flats moved in, trying front doors, peering through the windows of the empty houses, seeing what they could pick up. Joey went with them. He

wasn't in the gang. He wished he was, and trailed along behind. They let him do this because Joey had sharp eyes. He could find things other people missed. When he found something, Pogger would look it over and decide whether to take it away from Joey. And Joey said nothing because he was a bit afraid.

This Saturday morning, the gang was poking around one of the backyards, where the gate hung open. Suddenly Joey spotted something wedged between two stones near the battered old dustbin. He picked it up. It was small and grey, even black in parts. But it was flat, round and it felt like money. He rubbed it and the tiniest gleam of silver showed through.

"What've you got there?"

Joey tried to slip it into his pocket. But Pogger stood over him, hands held out. The others gathered round. Joey straightened up. He kept the coin in his fingers but held it up. He faced Pogger timidly.

"It's an old coin," he began. He didn't say, "It might be worth something," because Pogger would snatch it.

He waited. Pogger looked Joey's find over.

"Huh. Rubbish."

"Tisn't. It's ..." Joey burst out, then stopped. He didn't like being sneered at but he didn't want Pogger to get too interested.

"It's what?" demanded Pogger.

"It's worth – something," answered Joey lamely.

"How much?"

Joey shrugged. The others laughed.

"All right. If it's worth something, flog it to old Hardacre. We'll go with you and see how much."

Pogger looked cunning. Joey knew what that meant. But he was caught. He couldn't back down now and say it was rubbish.

Reluctantly he followed Pogger and the gang down to

Hardacre's shop. The shop was closed. Joey's hopes rose.

"Perhaps it's shut. Perhaps he's moved out."

"Get off!" Pogger pushed the door open. Inside the bell clanged so loudly they stopped, then crowded up to the counter. In the dim light, the walls and shelves seemed to be crammed with objects like those in the window. Everywhere was still.

"Shop! Let's be having you!" called Pogger boldly. The others laughed and pushed each other.

"That'll do." The sharp words from the gloom behind the counter silenced them. There was Mr Hardacre, black suit, white hair, black patch and all, one sharp blue eye glaring at them.

"Well?"

No one spoke. Then Pogger nudged Joey.

"Go on. Ask him."

Joey, pressed up to the counter by the other boys, held out his coin. The shopkeeper's old hands, gnarled and blue veined, took it from him, studied it, then placed it on the counter.

"What's it worth, Mister?" Joey stammered. Mr Hardacre looked at him a moment, then ran his eye over the gang.

"That?" The others started to snigger. "That, sonny, is a Joey."

Now the others began to laugh. Joey turned red. Mr Hardacre opened a drawer under the counter, took out a canvas bag and slid three shining coins, one by one, on to the counter.

"This is money how it used to be before they decimalised it," he said. "Now that," he placed a finger on the largest, "is a bob, a door nob, a Barney Dillon, a Thomas Tilling, a shilling."

"That's 5p," began Pogger, scornfully, and then was silenced by Mr Hardacre's blue eye. Down came another coin.

"That's a Lord of the Manor, a Tartan Banner, a tanner, a sixpence. Worth half as much as the other."

"Two and a half pee," Pogger added impudently.

Lastly, Mr Hardacre placed next to Joey's grubby little piece, a shining coin of the same size. "And here we have a Dora Gray, an un, deux tray, a thrum, a kettle drum, a threepenny Joey, and that's worth just half as much as the last one."

There was a second's silence while the gang took this in then one of them crowed, "One and a quarter pee. That's what Joey's worth."

Now the others fell about and punched each other, while Joey looked for a crack in the floor he could vanish through. Then Pogger took charge.

"Come on!" He headed for the door and the others crowded after him. Crestfallen, Joey looked at his threepenny bit on the counter. Then he shrugged. It wasn't worth much but at least he still had it. He reached out to pick it up and saw Mr Hardacre looking at him. The blue eye seemed milder.

"Is that really all it's worth, Mister?" Joey asked.

"Worth and worth . . ." the old man cocked his head towards the door which had closed on Pogger's gang. "That's good enough for the rabble. But," he paused, "you and I know different."

Mr Hardacre turned away a moment and when he turned back to the counter he had a small jeweller's eye glass fixed over his good eye. Now he looked stranger still but his voice was solemn.

"This is a real silver Joey. Eighty years old if it's a day. That's how they made 'em. Point nine-two-five fine, almost pure silver." He nodded. "Later on when the price of silver went up, it cost more to make these little coins than the value they had stamped on them. Imagine that, Joey, making money and losing on it." He chuckled. "So they started mixing in copper and nickel and all that muck. But this one, lad, is the real gubbins." Mr Hardacre turned the coin in his fingers. "That's why it's gone black here and there."

He reached down and took a rag and bottle out of the drawer under the counter and began delicately to touch the metal which now began to gleam.

"See – the obverse side, with the King's head. King George the fifth." Joey stared.

"The Queen's grandad, son."

"So, what's it worth then, Mister?" Joey asked eagerly.

Mr Hardacre's tone changed. He spoke formally.

"As silver, scrap silver, sir? Well, at 28 quid an ounce, I can offer you two pounds, say." Joey's face fell. Two pounds was something. But he'd expected more. Mr Hardacre smiled.

"Let's look on the reverse." He turned and rubbed at the coin. "Look at that."

Joey saw the figure three, then smaller, 1911.

"Now, a coin dealer might give you seven, eight quid for that. It's in good nick. Not extremely fine, but very fine, I should say." Joey's eyes grew round.

"Wait a bit." The old man's voice changed once more almost as if he were excited.

"Lookt'ee. That crown over the three. This one comes out of a Maundy set. Tha knows, son, old folk used to get 'em as a gift from Royalty, on Maundy Thursday, before Easter. Wait a bit, now."

The old man put down the coin and rag and hurried into the back of the shop. He was gone some time and Joey grew impatient. Then he was back, carrying a little leather case.

"This was my Grandad's Maundy set." He opened the case. Inside were three shining silver coins, and a small empty socket in the lining. "Fourpence, twopence, one penny. But all silver. Very special."

Now Joey was excited. "The threepenny bit's missing."

Impulsively he took his coin and started to fit it into the empty space, then stopped.

"Hey. D'you reckon my coin's really your missing one?" The old man shook his head, then laughed as if at himself.

"If you promise to say nowt, Joey, I'll tell you what happened to that missing threepence." He leant across the counter and lowered his voice. "I pinched it, out of our Grandad's case." Joey stared.

"When I was your age, Joey, my pocket money, when I got any, were ha'penny a week. Can you imagine, a threepenny bit – six weeks' pocket money all at once. I knew the shopkeeper wouldn't take a silver fourpence or a twopence or a penny. But a Maundy threepence looked almost the same as any other.

"So, I couldn't resist. I had away with it, and for a whole day I was cock of the walk down our street. I bought a penny bag of chips and peas, you got a lot for a penny. I shared 'em out among the chosen few. Then ha'penny on a roll of Spanish – that's like a liquorice strip. I shared that out as well. Then ha'penny on a bag of sherbet. I ate all that myself. And with my last penny I bought a Rover comic off one of my mates. Then I swapped it for a Wizard comic, then swapped that for a Champion, and so on. They were grand stories. Deadwood Dick, Strang the Terrible, the Wolf of Kabul." Mr Hardacre's voice sounded far away.

"I'll never forget it. But it couldn't last. They found out." Joey nodded. They always do.

"Our Dad was going to leather me. 'I'll tan the hide off him,' he shouted. I hid in the coal hole and wouldn't come out. But Grandad laughed. Did he laugh. 'Give over,' he told our Dad. 'It's only threepence. Not worth all that fuss. Anyway, I reckon he'll never do that again.'" Mr Hardacre smiled again at the memory.

"They tried to get that threepenny bit back from the shop, but it had gone out again as change. They never found it. Grandad left the set, such as it was, to our Dad, and he left it to me."

Mr Hardacre took the coin from Joey and popped it into the empty space. "If that set were complete, and if I wanted to sell they'd give £40 to £50." Joey looked up at Mr Hardacre.

"As much as that?" The old man looked embarrassed, then serious.

"Wouldn't do, Joey. See."

He picked up a sharp pointed tool and picked at the coin with it. A piece of grit fell down on to the counter. Then he showed the coin to Joey. A hole had been drilled through near the rim.

"It's been pierced. Dealers don't like that. Some people will plug a pierced coin with tin, and silver it over just to sell it." Joey smiled. Mr Hardacre went on.

"But somebody thought it was worth keeping, Joey. They hung it round their neck."

On impulse, Joey said, "Would you like it any road. To make up your set?"

The old man shook his head.

"Get away Joey. It's yours, if it's anybody's. Besides, if I put your coin in there it looks as if I'm trying to hide my guilty past, doesn't it?"

He fished in the drawer again and this time held up a length of nylon thread. He began to push this through the hole in the coin, then beckoned to Joey.

"Come here, lad."

Joey bent forward over the counter. Mr Hardacre fastened the thread, then slipped it over Joey's head and tucked the coin down the front of his shirt.

"That'll bring you luck, Joey. I know it." He winked his

single eye and nodded towards the door. "They'll not get their hands on it now, eh?"

Joey closed the shop door behind him. After the gloom inside, the morning sun was very bright. He strolled along, hands in pockets, thinking about everything Mr Hardacre had told him.

As he reached the flats he heard them laughing. Pogger and the gang were shouting:

"Threepenny Joey. Threepenny Joey." Joey took no notice. Smiling to himself he ran up the steps, leaving them staring after him.

THE MAN WITH THE SILVER TONGUE

by Rory McGrath

———

There was no doubt about it, Herbert Cragnut was born with a silver tongue. Anyone who met him when he was a young lad said, "Herbert, you have a silver tongue!" Now Herbert didn't really understand what people meant when they said this ... and just in case *you* don't, I'll tell you. If a person has a silver tongue it means that that person is a good talker or has a clear, sweet, melodious voice. Both these things were true of Herbert. But when he was a small boy, Herbert thought people meant that his tongue was actually made out of silver. And once when he was short of pocket money around Christmas time, he even went to a jewellers to have it valued.

"What can I do for you, little boy," asked the wizened but friendly old jeweller.

Herbert replied, "I want some money for this," and immediately stuck his tongue out.

"How dare you! Clear off," said the wizened but no longer friendly old jeweller. Herbert explained what he meant and the old man laughed and pointed out Herbert's misunderstanding. "You have a silver tongue, my boy, it's true. A beautiful clear voice. You should be an actor or a singer. You should be on stage or even in films!"

But that was a long, long time ago. Let's come up to date ... to a modern comprehensive school where Herbert was now a bitter and bad-tempered old English teacher ...

"I should have been an actor or a singer, I should have been on stage or even in the films ... and not just stuck here in this miserable school teaching you disgusting flea-ridden

malodorous troglodytes! Perkins, stop sniggering or I'll excoriate you till you scream for mercy."

"What does malodorous mean, sir?" asked one of the boys.

"What does troglodyte mean, sir, and excoriate?" asked another.

"What does Perkins mean?" asked Perkins cheekily.

"Right. Consider yourselves in a state of detention after school as just punition for this outrageous insurrection," said Herbert. What Herbert hated most in the world was school children. What school children hated most in the world was Herbert ... and, of course, sprouts.

Well, actually there was one pupil who quite liked Herbert and marvelled at his voice and his words. He was called Walker, but on account of his large sticky-out ears everyone called him "Lugs". Lugs would often stay behind and talk to Herbert about some of the long impressive sounding words. And of course Lugs realised that Herbert was in fact a very good teacher if only he didn't lose his temper so quickly and so often. Herbert was quite flattered by the youngster's attention and found that he didn't despise Lugs as much as the others.

But in general, though, Herbert would shout and scream insults at his pupils all day long and they would just smirk or snigger. This made him even more angry. The reason the kids sniggered, of course, was because they could never understand Herbert's insults. The silver-tongued schoolmaster used such long and complicated words that they meant nothing to the boys. He called them things like "scurrilous scrofulations", "putrescent amoebas", "coprophagous cretins" or "purulent prominences" and the boys and girls, well, they just shrugged their shoulders and laughed.

If he'd called them "spotty scumbags" or "snotfaced toe-rags" they might have shut up and had more respect for Herbert. But they had such contempt for Mr Cragnut that they didn't even bother thinking up a nickname for him. Oh, they had nicknames for the other teachers. The headmaster, for example, talked with a sizzling breathy voice and they called him "Hissing Sid". The chemistry teacher was a small man who always looked as if he'd just come out of a rainstorm, they called him "Dripdry", and there was the PE teacher who had been a policeman and who'd once had a metal plate inserted into his knee after an accident. They called him "Robocop". There were many others: "Dismal Desmond", "Humpy", "Ollie Beak", "Pizza-face Pratt", but as for Herbert Cragnut, they just called him Herbert. Or more often, that great big herbert, Herbert.

Herbert was annoyed that the children had been naughty. It meant he had to give them detention, which annoyed him because that meant *he* had to stay behind as well.

That annoyed him because it meant he missed his usual bus and had to get a rush hour bus and that annoyed him because the only seat that was left was upstairs. Now that doubly annoyed Herbert, firstly because the bus always started as he was only halfway up the stairs and he invariably lost his balance and fell backwards, lunging rather unflatteringly at the rail. Secondly going upstairs meant he had to sit in the smoking

section and smoking really annoyed Herbert.

"You ignorant plebs," he shouted as he sat down on the bus. "Kindly desist from your noxious exhalations. Do you not realise you are turning each molecule of our mutual atmosphere into a microscopic venomous projectile!"

"Sit down and shut up," shouted someone at the back.

An old lady whispered to her friend, "We always seem to get a nutter on the 134."

But the man next to him said, "Well said, I quite agree." But this man annoyed Herbert just as much because he had a silly moustache and a bow-tie. And Herbert hated those prissy vainglorious affectations!

He got home in a bad temper, he went to bed in a bad temper, he dreamed he was in a giant bad temper with sixteen floors and lots of windows. He woke up in a bad temper, had breakfast in a bad temper, shaved in a bad temper and had some tea in a . . . large blue and white cup.

But as he was leaving the house he noticed there was a message on the answerphone. "That's odd," he thought. "I turned the answerphone off before I went to bed." He pressed the playback button and listened. "BEEEEP I thought I'd better let you know I'm leaving you. Or rather I left you last night. I just got fed with all the bad temper and the shouting and the insults and the long words which no one understands, not even me! BEEEP!" Herbert was stunned! It was his voice on the answerphone.

"   !" said Herbert. "   !" He repeated.

Then a thought struck him. When he spoke just then nothing came out! It was just silence. And then the horror and the terror struck him. It wasn't *him* on the answerphone. It was his *voice*! His voice had left him.

He was still recovering from the shock a few hours later when he walked into the Police Station carrying a large box full of bits of card. His embarrassment was now cancelling out the shock of what had happened.

Shaking slightly he handed a card to the station sergeant who read what was on it.

"'I've ... lost ... my ... voice!' Oh I see, sir, well don't worry, just write everything down, no problem. What can we do for you?" Herbert handed the same card back to the policeman.

"'I've lost my voice'. Ah, listen, sir. I understand. I often lose my voice myself. Just write down what you've come to the Police Station for. Are you here to report something, to ask for something, to give us some information or what?" Herbert wrote something else on the card. The sergeant read it out!

"'I've lost my voice. That's it. Some people lose their dogs, I've lost my voice!'" The officer was perplexed. "You've lost

your voice like other people lose their dogs?" Herbert smiled and nodded. "So ... er ... your voice might have been run over by a car? Or it may have been stolen by a voice-lover who didn't already have a voice like yours? Or perhaps your voice got lost while chasing rabbits round the common?"

Herbert realised the policeman wasn't taking him seriously. He picked out another card from the box and handed it to the sergeant who read it out.

" 'I woke up this morning; my voice had gone. It left a message on the answerphone but it didn't say where it had gone!' " The sergeant was beginning to think that Herbert wasn't taking *him* seriously. He glanced up at the calendar to see if it was April the First. It wasn't. The sergeant was absolutely stumped; he didn't know what to do. So he resigned from the Police Force there and then and went off to live in Devon and grow tomatoes. That didn't help Herbert who was waiting at the Police Station front desk. A young bright-looking policeman walked in and Herbert handed him a card. The young constable read it.

" 'Have any voices been handed in?' Er ... I'll go and check," he said. After a few minutes he returned with three boxes. "Is it one of these?" asked the young PC, and he opened the first box. Herbert heard a voice come out of the box.

"I'll tell you what, son, it's been a terrible week for the nags. All this rain has made swamps of the courses," said a broad Irish accent. Herbert shook his head and the constable opened the second box. "Ninety-two years old I am, ninety-two. I can remember as far back as ... er ... when was it now ... nineteen something it was ... and the King, or possibly the Queen ..." the old croaky voice trailed off. Herbert shook his head again and they tried the third box. "Allo, m'sieu. Could you please tell me the best route to the Palace of Buckingham. I would like to see the guards being changed." Another blank. Herbert went home a sad and broken man.

Herbert couldn't possibly go back to school. He had to find his voice. So he drew his curtains and put a note on the door saying "Visiting a sick aunt in Australia. Back in a few weeks." By day he'd slip out in disguise in search of his voice. But in vain. He was distraught. He began thinking that even teaching school children was better than having no voice. He thought to himself, "If ever I get my voice back, I might start being nice to those little blighters!"

Meanwhile three of Herbert's pupils were playing in Bogle Cave a few miles from the town. They were Gary, Lee and Lugs. The stalactites and stalagmites made the three children feel they were inside the mouth of a giant shark surrounded by savage teeth.

"It's like being inside the mouth of a giant shark surrounded by savage teeth!" said Lugs.

"How do you know?" challenged Gary. "Have you ever been inside the mouth of a giant shark?"

"No," said Lugs.

"Well, shut up then," answered Gary.

"Stop arguing," said Lee. "Let's get out of here, I'm frightened!"

In truth, they were all a little bit frightened. Bogle Cave was a weird place. The walls glistened with slime and crawled with strange insects that had eerie glowing tails. The ceiling dripped constantly with freezing water and occasionally the torch light picked out the ugly shapes of sleeping bats hanging from the roof like leather rags.

"All right then, we'll go if you're scared," said Gary who was a bit superstitious and remembered that he'd read somewhere that bats swooped down on you and sucked blood from your neck and when you woke up you were a bat as well and couldn't see yourself in the mirror or eat garlic.

"Wait a minute," said Lugs. "We can't go until we've heard the echo! All caves have an echo. We've got to shout something. Hello!" shouted Lugs.

"Hello!" came the echo loud and clear.

"Goodbye," shouted Lee who was even more frightened now.

"Goodbye," shouted back the echo very distinctly.

Lugs shouted again. "My name is Mickey Walker but every-one calls me Lugs."

The echo came back immediately.

"I know!" The children stared at each other in horror. Then they screamed and ran for it!

"Help, help, help!" they cried.

"Don't go, don't go, don't go!" echoed the echo. But they had gone.

On his way home, Lugs couldn't stop thinking about the echo. It seemed to be not just an echo but a voice in its own right . . . and a fine deep voice too . . . and a voice he recognised. The voice of Herbert Cragnut.

Herbert picked up the note that was lying on the doormat. It was written in a hand he recognised. It was Lugs' writing. "Why don't you come back to school," the note said. "It can't be much fun hiding in Bogle Cave." Herbert, of course, hadn't been hiding in Bogle Cave at all. But he knew immediately what the note meant. His voice was hiding in Bogle Cave. He'd go there straight away and plead with his voice to come back. But how would he start a conversation with his voice without his voice. "I'll take the answerphone," he thought. "On it is a recording of me saying, 'Hello this is Herbert Cragnut.'" This was a very clever idea, he thought.

"Hello this is Herbert Cragnut," rang out the answerphone in the dank cave.

"Hello this is Herbert Cragnut," came the reply. Herbert tried it again a few times. Every time the echo came back the same. "Hello this is Herbert Cragnut." Herbert knew that the echo was really his voice so he decided to just sit there and wait for his voice to make the next move . . . or the next sound. After about half an hour the echo boomed through the cave.

"All right then. You win. It is me." Herbert smiled. "I

thought you'd find me eventually."

"   !" said Herbert.

"And tell me why I should come back," said Herbert's voice.

"   ," said Herbert.

"You can't live without me. Ha ha ha ha. Very funny," said Herbert's voice. "Well I can live without the constant angry shouting and insulting. I am a fine voice. I should be giving pleasure not pain!"

"   !" said Herbert.

"Of course, I'm right!" said Herbert's voice.

"   ," said Herbert.

"All right then, explain!" said Herbert's voice. So Herbert explained.

"   ." He explained how he'd set his heart on being an actor or a singer or some sort of entertainer when he was a boy but his parents said he was silly, that show business was a wicked and risky business and he should study hard and get a really sensible steady job like teaching. They were both teachers and they were comfortable and happy. Though Herbert never remembered them smiling a lot. They certainly never laughed. They wouldn't let him take part in the school plays; they wouldn't take him to the cinema or the theatre and wouldn't let him go on his own. He became an average boring teacher. He hated the children he taught. Especially the ones who had lovely voices, especially the ones who sang, especially the ones in the school play and of course the ones who chatted about the latest play or film their parents had taken them to see. His silver tongue had got tarnished. There was a nasty bitter taste in his mouth.

After hearing his tale Herbert's voice was speechless.

"I ... I ... just don't know what to say. I know, I'll make a deal with you," it said firmly.

"   !" said Herbert. So Herbert's voice outlined the deal and Herbert agreed. From now on Herbert Cragnut's beautiful voice would never be used in anger or insult. It was a very happy Herbert who sat on the top deck of the bus back into town. He and his voice were chatting amiably.

"It's really nice having you back. Well I'm looking forward to a happy partnership. So am I. I did miss you, you know. I bet you did."

The old woman in the seat behind turned to her friend and said, "We always seem to get a nutter on the 134."

Herbert didn't go back to teaching. He decided to do what he always wanted to do: become an entertainer and use his voice to the best of his ability. And in a short time he became one of the most popular entertainers in the country. Amusing for adults and delightful for children. Herbert Cragnut had become a ventriloquist. He had his dummy made especially with sticky out ears and called him Lugs in honour of the boy who'd helped him to find his voice. And when you saw him do his act with Lugs on his knee you'd swear that the voice was coming from the dummy, which spoke in a melodious, distinct, rich, fruity voice, while Herbert sat there not moving his lips at all. Sometimes he'd drink a glass of water and the dummy would still be talking ... sometimes he'd leave the stage altogether and the dummy would still be talking.

"Sorry about him," said the dummy. "He has to go home, it's way past his bedtime. I'll finish the show without him!" It was sensational. The audience was astounded. Herbert got into the finals of a national talent competition and out of two hundred entrants came a staggering second. Herbert didn't mind coming second. He actually preferred the runners-up medal which was, of course, silver!

HOLIDAY '66

by Trevor Neal and Simon Hickson

―――――――――

Welcome, Friend! Welcome to our World of the Strange! We live on a huge planet – Earth. A planet so huge, and yet, in this age of high-speed travel and technology, so small. Despite all our understanding of science and the Universe, there still remain many things of which we know very little indeed. And it is here, Friend, that our World of the Strange begins. It is our quest to investigate those mysteries for which answers have not yet been found.

Oh yes, Friend, read on as we unfold before your very eyes certain factual occurrences that will throw into question your whole perception of the world as you know it! Prepare, Friend, to be turned upside down – shaken – plunged into a swirling void of confusion. And then, Friend, hurled violently against the wall of disbelief!

Ha! But we hear the more cynical ones amongst you cry out, "Oh, that's fine dramatic language ..." (Thank you, we wrote it ourselves.) "... But you don't shock me." No? Wait and see, Friend, wait and see.

However, before we begin our tale of mystery, please ensure, Friend, that you are settled, relaxed and comfortable. We do not take kindly to interruptions. We insist that you tell your friends and your family that you must not be disturbed. (Why not make a paper hat with the words "Sssshhh! I'm in the World of the Strange!" written on it?)

Close the doors. Draw the curtains. Come closer, Friend. Draw nearer, closer.

Are you ready? Comfortable? Really? Positive? You don't

want to go to the toilet or anything? Let us begin.

It all began on a cold, wet winter's night. A Mr Mark Ree from Kent was driving home from work. Mr Ree was a sales manager for a small company who manufactured, amongst other things, battery operated portable hair dryers, ideal for the travelling business person.

His journey home was not unusual, Friend. A fifteen-mile drive, and one that he did five times a week. Mr Ree looked into his mirror as he casually drove along the crowded dual carriageway. He was checking a small patch on the top of his head to see if there was any sign of hair growing there.

The reason, Friend, is that several days earlier Mr Ree suffered a rather nasty accident when demonstrating the latest model in compact portable hair dryers to a buyer from a reputable chain of electrical goods shops. Mr Ree switched on the appliance planning to demonstrate its neat simplicity linked with its sleek good looks and surprisingly powerful jet of warm air.

However, on this strange day, the hair dryer instead of blowing, sucked, and took a large clump of Mr Ree's otherwise fine head of hair deep into the mechanism of the device.

The hair smouldered, the hair dryer buzzed, caught fire, exploded, sent a bright spark of hot hair flying into the back of a nearby video, blew the fuse, spread to the shop's entire display of videos, TVs, Hi-Fis, CDs, and threw the shop into a complete black hole of non-electrical darkness!

How could this happen? Why had the hair dryer sucked? Had there been a sudden and strange reversal in the laws of nature and relativity just as he had switched it on? Had a passing alien spaceship caused an inverse surge of power across the national electricity supply? Or was it just faulty wiring in a sub-standard cheap electrical appliance? Ponder on this, Friend, as we continue on our strange tale!

Meanwhile, Mr Ree, his hair now nearly back to normal, sat back and concentrated on the fifteen-mile drive ahead.

Mr Ree was, in fact, rather enjoying his drive home this night. The reason, Friend? Because it was his first real drive in his new car, a silver coloured 1300 hatchback. Mr Ree always fancied a silver coloured car as he felt it added that certain sporty feel to what was otherwise a sensible, practical family car.

Furthermore he had managed to purchase this particular model at a bargain price from Dave's Used Cars. Mr Ree had checked in a bi-monthly car magazine and had discovered that a car of this kind was worth at least £500 more than the amount he had just given to Dave. What's more, Friend, the car had incredibly low mileage. Although it was three years old it had only done 5000 miles. Such low mileage for a car of that age was quite unbelievable! And the paintwork was immaculate. There was not a scratch on it. A car of this age would normally have the odd bump, dent or scratch; but no, the car appeared to be flawless, as if, Friend, it had just been sprayed.

Mr Ree was very content. Dave's Used Cars obviously didn't know much about the second-hand car business, that much was clear! A new car, a day's work finished, not too much hair missing, and a rather interesting programme on the radio all about the career of the popular rock group, Dire Straits. Mr Ree, singing along to the chorus of "The Walk of Life", was very content indeed.

Then his car blew up! Well no, Friend, perhaps we have over-dramatised the situation. A loud crunching sound came from the engine. It spluttered and stalled. Inside the car Mark Knopfler crackled, made a loud rude noise, and then went silent as the radio ceased to function. "Oh well," thought Mr Ree, "better ring the AA, I suppose." Then all four wheels fell off, a large crack opened in the roof of the car, the doors fell off and crashed to the ground. A thin jet of steam gushed from the radiator and the steering wheel fell into Mr Ree's lap. The car alarm emitted a high-pitched whistle attracting fourteen dogs from the locality: nine rottweilers, three dobermans, one bull terrier and a shih-tzu.

Two hours later a very nice man, an AA man, arrived at the sad scene. Mr Ree, by now a broken man, sat in a crumpled heap. The AA man convinced Mr Ree that there was nothing to be gained from crying like a baby, and then he began his examination of the car.

What happened, Friend? How strange that a car which Mr Ree had only just bought, with as little as 5000 miles on the clock, should just fall to pieces. Yet again Mr Ree found himself the victim of bizarre forces beyond his control!

The AA man finished his examination. He informed Mr Ree that the engine in his car was not that of a 1300 hatchback, but the engine of a local council lawn mower! Strange indeed! However, under further scrutiny the AA man revealed that the body of Mr Ree's car was in fact made from the bodies of two different cars. One half was indeed a hatchback, but the other half, Friend, was the body of a 1979 three-wheeler!

Furthermore, it could now be seen that neither of these cars were originally silver coloured. The bright mauve paintwork of the former three-wheeler shone through the chipped silver and evidence of what used to be a leaf green hatchback could also be witnessed quite clearly.

Mr Ree was stunned. How could this have happened, Friend? Was Mr Ree the unfortunate victim of an extra-terrestrial interplanetary car-swopping experiment? Had he passed through a matter-transformation zone just past junction

13 on the M25? Had he entered it just as a 1979 three-wheeler passed in the opposite direction, fusing them together in a cosmic exchange of swirling molecules and gaskets? Or had he just been badly ripped off by Dave, the used car salesman? All we know is that Mr Ree's life was getting stranger by the hour and no amount of logic or reason could prepare our poor unfortunate victim for the fate which beheld him upon arriving home.

As Mr Ree approached his front door he heard a shrill ringing coming from within his home. What do you think it was? A visitor from a distant galaxy trying to communicate in its native language? ... No, don't be silly, Friend, it was just the telephone, of course!

Unfortunately Mr Ree got to his telephone too late. But there was a message awaiting him on his answerphone; a strange message which confused and disturbed him. It was the voice of his boss who had just been notified of Mr Ree's unfortunate accident with the sucking hair dryer – the accident which had led to Mr Ree's company losing a £100,000 contract with a respectable electrical goods store. His boss sounded strange, different from usual. In a deep, serious, yet almost quivering tone, the voice conveyed this message: "Why not take a long holiday, Mark! Just go away for a while, and don't come back!" The message ended rather abruptly.

"How strange," thought Mr Ree. Why was he being offered a long holiday when he had only been in the job for two weeks? And why did his boss sound as if a strange force had invaded his soul? For the first time it occurred to Mr Ree that he had recently experienced an extraordinary amount of bad luck. Was he just a clumsy, stupid idiot, or was he at the centre of a terrifying conspiracy bent on making his life a living hell? Mr Ree laughed to himself. Of course his boss wasn't trying to sack him. He obviously had his best interests at heart, and Mr

Ree had to agree with him, he did need a holiday.

Later that same evening, Mr Ree filled his mind with thoughts of rest, relaxation and holidays. Suddenly he remembered a place he had been to as a child, a small seaside village called Silverdale. There he had spent a smashing summer holiday with his parents, in 1966. A tiny village with a few shops, Silverdale also had a small harbour with fishing boats and a nice little beach about half a mile down the coast. What a fun time he'd had then. Fishing every day, he remembered catching a bass on the Monday, a mullet on Tuesday, an eel on Wednesday, and he'd lost count of all the crabs he had caught. That was what he needed! A good rest at the seaside, fishing, walking, chatting to the local villagers. He made up his mind to go the very next day, and fell into a deep sleep dreaming of fishing, walking and chatting to the local villagers.

The following morning at the crack of dawn, he packed his suitcase. Six pairs of socks, six pairs of underpants, six shirts, six toothbrushes, six tubes of toothpaste. Then he took out five of the toothbrushes and toothpaste tubes; he would only need one of each. He packed his swimming trunks, the blue and yellow striped ones with a picture of swordfish on them. The thought of jumping into the lovely fresh sea at the golden beach of Silverdale after all these years filled Mr Ree with joy and excitement.

Mr Ree put his suitcase into the boot of his car. He then took it out again, remembering that his car was a heap of junk, and walked to the train station.

"Return to Silverdale, please!"

"Where?" snapped the uniformed man behind the counter. "There's no such place!"

"Yes there is. It's near Gosfroth."

"Oh, Gosfroth. Why didn't you say so in the first place? It's an 'Off White with a Hint of Blue' Saver Day, so that's £152 please. Thank you. Goodbye."

Arriving at Gosfroth station, three hours and one chocolate chip cookie later, Mr Ree hired a bicycle and set off on the twelve-mile journey to Silverdale.

Now, Friend, you may have noticed that things are going remarkably well for Mr Ree. You may be thinking, "What's so strange about this tale?" You may be thinking, "Sure, it began strangely enough, but now it's becoming nothing more than a rather mundane travelogue. Perhaps I should take off my 'Sssshhh, I'm in the World of the Strange' paper hat and put on my 'Ah I'm in the World of Make Myself a Cup of Tea' hat instead." But, Friend, do not be so hasty. Read on and prepare yourself for an astounding development.

Mr Ree unfolded a local map and found that Silverdale was no longer there. Had his memory failed him? No, Friend, for on the map were other places he remembered only too well. Places like the village of Bunyon, the little hamlet of Wigerling, and Toot Pond. But where was Silverdale? And why were the roadsigns that twenty-five years ago pointed to Silverdale, now replaced by roadsigns pointing to a place called Silvervalley Industrial Park?

With nowhere else to go, and still thinking there must be a mistake, Mr Ree headed down that road. The road that he knew would bring him face to face with his fond memories of fishing, walking and chatting with the local villagers!

Turning left at the crossroads in Bunyon, Mr Ree headed down the country lane which would take him the last five miles into Silverdale – five miles of beautiful countryside, splendid views and the glory of the sparkling sea. But no, Friend, this wasn't the sight that greeted his eyes. Oh no, the only thing that greeted Mr Ree was the stinking stench of acrid pollution. Oh yes the little harbour of Silverdale, with its quaint fishing boats, friendly fishermen, and mullets, was now a heaving mass of chemical waste, toxic fumes, belching smoke and Portakabin toilets. Silverdale had become Silvervalley Industrial Park!

Mr Ree did go fishing. But did he catch a bass? Did he catch a mullet? An eel? No, Friend. Instead he caught a rather nasty skin disease which broke out in a big rash all over his body.

Mr Ree did go walking. However, he found himself walking headlong into stagnant cesspools of chemical sludge, on top of which bobbed little bits of polystyrene and plastic containers.

And yes, Friend, Mr Ree did indeed try talking to the local villagers, but the only one he could find was wearing a hard hat, protective face mask and a white boiler suit. Instead of pleasantly passing the time of day in lighthearted conversation, this rude villager pointed at a large board which stated:

GO AWAY! GET OUT! KEEP CLEAR! DON'T TELL ANYONE WHAT YOU'VE SEEN AND DON'T COME BACK ... OR ELSE, NOSEY!

THANK YOU FOR YOUR CO-OPERATION! NOW GET LOST!

Confused and distressed by this tragic turn of events Mr Ree made a hasty retreat!

What had happened? Had Silverdale been invaded by rampaging alien hordes who had come from the Moon? And what about the pools of sludge? Were they vital supplies of Alien Juice ready to be pumped into nearby squadrons of battlestar intergalactic fighting forces? And the man in the white suit? A local villager? Or the infamous Warlord, Viscosian, hellbent on massive destruction on an inhuman scale?

No, Friend, it was none of these – unfortunately. It's just the way things are these days. Mr Ree's memory did serve him correctly. In 1966 Silverdale was a beautiful seaside resort, ideal for fishing, walking and chatting to the local villagers! But now ... it's just a bit of a dump.

So, Friend, you may be asking yourself, why has this tale been included in the World of the Strange when the events described have nothing more than everyday occurrences? Well there is yet one more strange development in our tale! Mr Ree did not return home that night, nor the night after, or the night after that. What had become of him?

The reason is simple, Friend. The bicycle Mr Ree had hired earlier that day was not a bicycle at all, but an advanced spacecraft programmed to kidnap unsuspecting tourists and whisk them off to a planet many, many light years away, in a different solar system! Or at least, that is our belief.

SKULDUGGERY

by Tony Robinson

———

I stood on the threshold of my new school, heartily proud of my uniform. A red spotted handkerchief was tied jauntily round my head, my mole-skin sea boots were spick and span as was my buckled belt and golden ear-ring, and my blue and white striped shirt had not a single blood-stain on it. "Squire Trelawney's Academy for Young Sea-Dogs" announced the creaky sign above my head. "Head Teacher – Mistress Baker". 'Twas my first day at pirate school and my heart quickened as I swung my sea-chest upon my shoulder and pushed open the great wooden gates.

But pride turned to dismay at what I saw before me. There were no planks for walk-the-plank classes, no yard-arms from whence to hang one's foes, only a common playground like any other playground full of small groups of young students

garbed in white shirts, red ties and grey flannel trousers – and horror upon horrors, some of them were playing with yo-yos.

And then I beheld it, fluttering merrily from some unseen mast behind the crumbling school building: a skull and cross-bones – the flag which causes every pirate to swell with pride at his calling. I skirted round the school, 'twixt a motley collection of dustbins and a small hut bearing the words "Drama Studio", and there ahead of me was a small harbour, tied to the quay of which was the sweetest two-hundred-ton schooner I had ever seen.

I raced up the gangplank and opened a hatch ... below decks stank of skulduggery. Cautiously I descended a creaky flight of steps into the darkness below. Smoke-stained beams brushed my head, groaning timbers echoed down the gangways. Then Dee-dump! Dee-dump! Ahead of me I heard an eerie limping sound. Dee-dump! Dee-dump! My blood froze as it approached me. I flattened myself against the greasy oak wall and started as I felt a lump in the small of my back. When my initial terror subsided I discovered it was a door handle. On turning it, a door swung silently open. I stepped into a pitch black cabin and waited. The halting step approached my hiding place, paused, then moved off again. I was safe.

"Gotcha!" A hand clawed at my face.

"Snoopin' were ye?" Two more hands grabbed my arms and wrenched them tight behind my back sending my chest crashing to the ground. I was being inspected by two of the foulest young schoolboys I had ever seen. One had the face of a skeleton and spectacles with lenses six inches thick; the other was a pale tallowy creature with a bandage round two fingers of his left hand. I watched in horror as he began to poke my chest.

"Full of bits and baubles, I'll be bound," sneered the other.

"Nay, two silver handled pistols, a tinder from the Indies

and my father's priceless treasure maps," I retorted recklessly and glanced down at the key I kept secreted on a chain round my neck. In a trice eight broken finger nails and a bandage tore it from me. I cried out in despair. My first day, and my dearest possessions were to be lost.

At that moment the room flooded with light.

"Near-sighted Pew! Black Dog!" snapped a haughty buxom woman. "How many times do I have to tell ye, this boat is out of bounds! Now, return the chest and key at once!" Sullenly the rogues obeyed.

"Sorry, mistress," they whined. "We thought 'e were a-trespassing," and they slunk off into the shadows.

"You must be Ben," continued the headmistress, for indeed it was she. "Take no heed of Pew. He's a kindly boy really. Indeed, I have arranged for you to share a study. Come, I'll show you the lie of the land."

We left the schooner and proceeded across the harbour.

"You join us at a time of high excitement," she said proudly. "In order to place the school on a sound financial basis, this quay is to be transformed. In three weeks it will no longer be a grubby backwater, 'twill become 'Squire Trelawney's Pirate World'. Folk will come from far and wide to witness how the world once was when pirates sailed the Spanish Main. In

exchange for two pieces of silver they will play at pirates for a whole day with free lunch and a trip round the harbour included."

"Play at pirates!" I protested. "But pirating's a serious business."

"Indeed it is," my headmistress affirmed. "But times have changed, schools have no money and pirates must learn new skills."

As we entered the school, I saw how she was minded. Her young charges neither drank rum nor sang sea-shanties. They were engrossed in books on business studies and property markets, while their teachers lectured them on banking and the law of contracts.

"If my school is to succeed it must produce pirates for today's world," she said. "That is the purpose of modern education."

After exchanging my garb for more suitable grey flannels, she left me outside the door of the odious Pew. I knocked, swallowed hard and entered. A figure rocked gently back and forth in a hammock. I waited for a renewed attack upon my chest but none came.

"Shiver me timbers!" chuckled a friendly voice. "It's the new sea-pup!" The character who had confronted me was about twelve years old with intelligent eyes and a face like a ham. He pulled himself up in his hammock and took my hand in his firm grasp.

"Short John Silver at your service," he said by way of introduction.

"But I'm to share with Near-Sighted Pew," I stuttered.

"Well, Pew's a slippery swab," he retorted, "and I believe the pair of ye have already had a tidy set-to, so I thought to meself, let honest John be young Ben's shipmate."

I was mightily reassured by this invitation and told my new

friend how fearful I was of Pew's designs upon my chest. Lazily Silver leant over and pressed a panel in the wall. Silently it slid open to reveal a large hidey-hole.

"Stow it here," he said. "It'll be our little secret, eh? As snug as a crab in a cockle shell."

I sat enthralled while he told me tales of his adventures in the workhouse and at reform school, until a bell sounded and I hastened back to the quay where Mistress Baker was to inform me of my duties. I was a mite aggrieved to discover there was to be no fencing practice nor keel-hauling. Instead I was obliged to assist in the construction of a box-office for the Pirate World. Though I would rather have been swinging across a man-o'-war with a dagger between my teeth, the tasks were pleasing enough, particularly the numbering of the tickets, and by evening, tired and satisfied with my labours, I hastened back to my room eager for more of Silver's yarns. But no smiling face welcomed me. I was greeted only by an empty hidey-hole. Short John's assistance had been in vain.

I scoured the school for assistance or a glimpse of the cowardly Pew, until my searchings were rewarded by the sight of my two foes scuttling towards the schooner. And in their hands were a hammer, a chisel and my late father's sea-chest.

Across the quay I crept and once more boarded the ship. A shaft of light from below deck indicated the direction the odious pair had taken. With a cunning knife I had purchased from a captain in the Swiss Army, I prised two planks minutely apart and applied my eye to the hole. Below me was an unforgettable sight: a secret room brimful of pirates' apparel – hats, boots, hooks and eye-patches – and piles of vicious weaponry – cutlasses, scimitars, double-headed boarding axes. And in the midst of this buccaneers' bounty stood Pew and Black Dog hacking at my chest. Then a dreadful familiar sound caused them to arrest their activities. Dee-dump! Dee-dump! The limping figure approached them, obscured by shadows.

"We've a-lifted 'is box, Cap'n," whispered Black Dog.

"That snivellin' sea-slug'll be crying 'is-self to sleep for loss of it," added Pew, who was clearly no judge of character. "Our little plan's a-comin' on a treat."

The third figure spoke no words but softly whistled "Fifteen Men on a Dead Man's Chest". My curiosity knew no bounds. Who was this mysterious captain to whom even the most obnoxious schoolboys owed allegiance? I prised my hole wide open to catch a sight of his face, but unluckily at that moment Black Dog, who had resumed chiselling, took a severe blow on the thumb with his hammer. He threw his head back in pain, swearing mightily, and on seeing my face above him redoubled his curses and hurled the hammer in my direction. To my relief its force was broken by an overhanging stuffed parrot and I ran for dear life across the boat. I must find Mistress Baker and warn her that a dastardly plan was being hatched right under her poop deck.

I was about to knock on her study door when a cry from within caused me to pause.

"Spare me, Squire!" The headmistress was weeping uncontrollably.

"'Tis not I, Mistress Baker, 'tis the law," replied a gruff, heartless voice. "If the school cannot make money, it must be closed tomorrow."

"But I'm putting it on a business footing," Mistress Baker cried. "Once Pirate World is opened I will even have the wherewithal to purchase textbooks for the new curriculum."

"Once Pirate World is opened," crowed the Squire, "I won't need a school. I'll flatten it and use the site to park the visitors' carriages."

"Wait!" the hapless headmistress pleaded. "I have a new boy, a foolish prig who knows not his head from a packet of lard. He has a sea-chest containing a pair of silver pistols. I'll confiscate them and give them to you if only you'll spare my school. What do you say?"

I did not wait to hear the Squire's answer. I was surrounded by villains; even Mistress Baker was after the contents of my chest. I must seek out my one friend in the world – Short John Silver.

I sped to our study and slammed the door behind me.

"Gotcha again!" It was the loathsome voice of Black Dog. I cursed myself for the ass I had been. In my haste I had failed to observe my two enemies secreted on either side of the entrance.

"The treasure maps – where are they? You took 'em out the box, didn't ye?" hissed Near-Sighted Pew, twisting my arm and causing my eyes to water.

"Aye, that I did. And stored them cunningly where you will never find them," I retorted with all the bravery I could muster.

And then, Dee-dump! Dee-dump! I heard the dread sound approaching like the last judgement.

"'Tis the cap'n," grinned Black Dog wolfishly. "He'll

winkle out their whereabouts, by thunder!"

The door opened and, to my amazement, all was revealed. I had never seen Short John Silver standing up before, and there he was, one leg of human flesh, the other completely absent, causing him to walk with the aid of an enormous crutch. And, wonders of wonders, he was carrying my treasure maps.

"How in the name of Lucifer did you find them?" I gasped.

"They were under your pillow, dolt," replied my erstwhile friend. "A drunken cuttlefish could have devised a better hiding-place. Take 'em, boys, and if you blab to Mistress Baker, Ben, 'tis Davy Jones' Locker for you."

Fear gripped my heart. I wanted my own locker, not someone else's.

"Mistress Baker would prove no assistance," I retorted. "She too desires my chest. For the Squire will close the school tomorrow unless she finds some means of providing him with money."

"Tomorrow!" exploded my assailants in horror. Then Silver propelled himself out of the room and down the corridor bawling, "Israel Hands, Billy Bones, Job Anderson, stir yourselves from your slumbers! New orders, we sail tonight!"

Even as he spoke, boys burst from their rooms and followed him hotfoot to the ship, discarding their ties, shirts and flannel trousers as they ran. Soon twenty lads were racing up the gangplank dressed only in their under-garments. Hotfoot I pursued them, desperate for my chest. They dived below deck and in a trice had garbed themselves in their pirate's wear. No longer was I surrounded by school children. Nay, twenty fearsome buccaneers were now swarming up the rigging.

"We had planned this little jaunt for three weeks hence," yelled Short John, who was now miraculously transformed into a pirate captain. "Let modern schooling go hang: what need we of fancy Pirate Worlds when the high seas beckon? May Baker and her business schemes rot in hell. With your treasure maps to guide us we will sail the seven seas and bow and scrape to no man. Are you with us, Ben, or shall we toss you to the sharks?''

Before I could consider my answer, I spied Mistress Baker hastening across the quay calling, ''Come back, boys – remember your education!'' The ship strained at its mooring rope. I lifted a cutlass to hack it through. ''Not you too, Ben Gunn,'' she bellowed. ''I have need of your pistols.''

I brought the blade down with a crash. The boat swung seawards, the sails billowed, the crew began to sing a haunting pirate melody. Short John Silver put his arm round my shoulder and once more bestowed a smile upon me.

''Ben Gunn,'' he said, ''we'll be the best of mates for ever and ever.'' And looking into his clear blue eyes I knew that he would never let me down.

And was I correct to trust my friend? Read Treasure Island *by Robert Louis Stevenson and discover the answer.*

FISH TALE

by Nick Wilton

———

Holly was a chatterbox – everybody said that. At least they would have done if they could have got a word in edgeways. That was the main reason, if not the only reason, why her father always left her at home when he went fishing. Holly was convinced, however, that the reason he did not take her with him was because she was a girl. Although she was only six and a half years old she had already found out that there were some things that were usually done by boys and others that were done by girls.

Unfortunately, it seemed that girls were supposed to be Mummy's little helper, push plastic babies around in prams, and wear flowery dresses with frilly collars.

Holly didn't do any of these things. Well, she did try to help her Mum, but she asked so many questions that after three minutes her Mum would say that perhaps she could manage better without Holly's help, and why didn't she take her "baby" for a walk around the garden. Boys did much more exciting things like playing football, getting dirty and going fishing with Dad.

"It's nothing to do with you being a girl. It's just that, well, you'll get bored."

"I wouldn't, Dad. Honest."

"You couldn't keep still for eight hours."

"I could."

"AND quiet?"

"I could . . . well, I could try." So they had a test. Dad said if Holly could keep quiet for one hour while he washed the car (one of those things that dads usually do) she could go fishing with him. Holly did very well – for the first five minutes – and then she asked, "How long have I had now,

Holly was disappointed that yet again she would not be going fishing, but at least she knew she still had something to look forward to at the weekend.

Every Saturday when Dad went fishing, Holly and her Mum would go over to see her aunt and cousins. They had a wonderful garden with lots of secret places and very effective double glazing. So while her Mum and Aunty Lynn enjoyed peace and quiet inside, Holly, Lucy, Emily and Sophie enjoyed the opposite outside.

This weekend was going to be even better. Holly's Mum was off on a day trip to France with her French night school class, so Holly was staying overnight with her cousins. That was the plan anyway.

"It's typical," said Dad. "Why do they have to go and get ill this weekend? I mean, next week's the end of the season.

Next week would be fine."

"I don't think they've done it deliberately. I'm sure they'd rather not be ill at all."

"It's such a shame," Dad sighed.

"Yes, I'm really sorry, darling."

"You'll just have to cancel your trip and go another time," Dad continued.

"What?"

"Well, it's the big competition this weekend."

"That's okay, Dad. I can come fishing with you."

Holly had been listening at the door, even though she had been told not to several times in the past. "Two rods are better than one, and I can pack myself a box of sandwiches and get some worms from the garden, but I'll have to make sure I don't get the boxes mixed up. Mind you it's not as if I'm taking spaghetti. I mean it's easy to tell the difference between worms and sandwiches, but spaghetti looks a bit like worms only without the tomato sauce. The worms that is. I wonder if the fish could tell the difference, because I don't really fancy digging up worms. Have we got any spaghetti, Mum?"

"Maggots," said Dad.

"What?" Holly and Mum chorused.

"I don't use worms, I use maggots, and no, you're not coming with me. I'm sorry Holly, but no. And that's my final word."

Dad was right. It was indeed his final word. Mum went to France leaving Holly with him, and she just didn't stop talking. She talked more than ever, which you would think was imposs- ible, but then, she was very excited. Actually Dad got caught up in her excitement. They even made her a rod out of an old bit of bamboo, and tied some line to the end of it and a bent paperclip for a hook. But Holly would not be fishing for real; when she saw the maggots she decided that perhaps she would just watch.

In the end Dad was quite looking forward to her company. Mind you, he'd forgotten what she was like.

"Look, there's one! I'm sure I just saw one! Look there! Is that a fish, Dad, is that a fish?"

"No," said Dad for the seventy-fifth time. "Now why don't you take your sandwiches to that tree stump over there and have a picnic."

"I've already eaten them all." It never failed to amaze her father how Holly managed to eat, yet didn't seem to stop talking, but he let it pass, because at that moment he felt the rod twitch. Holly sensed that something was about to happen.

"About time too," she thought. They'd been there three hours and the most exciting thing that had happened so far was when she accidentally knocked over the maggots and they had to pick them up. Actually that wasn't really what you'd call exciting, more like disgusting.

"Dad, what is it? Is it a fish?"

"Mm."

Dad was concentrating on reeling in the line. He could already see his name on the cup. "Burgate Angling Association Competition Winner 1991."

"Dad, is it a fish?" Holly repeated, slightly louder. This was it. Full concentration now. "We've caught a fish! We've caught a fish!" sang Holly, as she danced up and down the bank. And yes, she did knock the maggots over again. But she didn't notice. Dad turned to shush her, which was probably a mistake.

"Oh no, it's gone in the weeds now. Holly, give me the net."

"There it is. I can see it, Dad, look. It's silver!"

"Yes, now pass me the net."

"That's amazing – a silver fish."

"It's just the light shining on it. Now give me the net." Holly

stood speechless, searching the weeds for another glimpse of the silver fish. "All right Holly, you hold the rod while I fetch the net. Don't touch the reel."

Holly took the rod from her father and as soon as his back was turned she released the ratchet on the reel. The line raced away, cutting through the water as a flash of silver darted out from the weeds.

"Quick, give me the rod! It's getting away!" said Dad, throwing down the net. "The ratchet must have slipped."

He started furiously reeling in the line but it was too late. Finally, the hook plopped out of the water. Empty.

"I just don't understand it. The reel's never done that before. Did you see it though? It must have been a good nine pounds. I reckon I could have won the competition with that. Did you see it? A good eleven pounds at least."

"It was silver," said Holly.

"What?"

"The fish. It was silver."

"Yes, it was a chub I think. A good size too. Maybe a thirteen pounder. I could have won Best of Season with that."

"No it was real silver. That's why I let it go."

"No, darling, it wasn't real sil ... you did what?"

Holly wandered along the river bank towards the old wooden bridge, feeling rather stupid. Of course it wasn't silver, well not real silver. It was just the light reflecting on its scales. If it had been silver it wouldn't float. It would just sink to the bottom and stay there. Poor old Dad. It would have been the biggest chub he'd ever caught. By the time he sent Holly off it was already over fifteen pounds. Well on the way to being a real all-time winner.

"And be careful you don't fall in," Dad had said, banishing her to the bridge, "you'll frighten what's left of the fish ... after that chub's warned all his friends off."

"Can they talk then, Dad?"

"Well no, but I should think they ..." But he wasn't going to be led into conversation that easily. He remembered just in time that he was meant to be angry. "Go on. Off you go."

As Holly kicked her way along the dusty towpath she looked for something she could throw in the river and fish out with the rod that Dad had made for her. It was a pity she hadn't thought of it before, this was going to be much more fun than watching Dad not catch fish.

Mind you, she wouldn't have seen her silver fish then, and that was worth the waiting. He was beautiful. She'd never seen a real fish before, only goldfish, which were rather small really, and those fish you see laid out on ice at the supermarket, but they were rather ugly – and dead, of course. Oh and smelly. She found some old plastic cups and the top of a flask, but then she thought she couldn't throw them into the river. That would make her as bad as the people who'd thrown them down in the first place. She popped them in a bin and looked for bits of wood instead.

Yes, this was going to be fun, she thought, as she stood on the bridge and threw the pieces of wood into the water. She was about to cast her line, as she'd seen Dad do, when she heard him shouting.

"Holly. Stop it!" Down the river bank Dad was waving his arms. "You'll worry the fish!" Holly dropped the remaining handful of sticks onto the bridge.

"Worry the fish?" she thought. "Not as much as getting a great big hook in the mouth, I bet."

"Pffft."

"Yes?" She looked round but there was nobody there. It must have been the wind.

"Pffft – over here." Over where? It seemed to be coming from the other side of the bridge. Holly started across cautiously, remembering what she had been told about talking to strangers, especially strangers who hid in bushes and went "Pssst". Or even "Pffft".

"Pffft." There it was again. "Here!"

Whatever it was it was in the rushes, but she couldn't see anything, only the sunlight catching an old bottle or something. "Oh," thought Holly, "it's just the breeze blowing across the top of an old bottle." But then she saw him.

"Oh, it's you – Silverfish."

"Who?"

"Oh, that's just my name for you. I know you're not really silver. I got a bit carried away that's all."

"Fo did I. On your Father'f fiffing line."

"Yes, I'm sorry about that – but wait a minute."

"I waffn't going anywhere," said Silverfish.

"You can talk."

"Huh, you can talk. Talk about talk. I've never heard fomeone talk af much af you."

"You talk funny though, don't you?"

"Do I?"

"Yes. All your S's sound like F's."

"Well having that hook in my mouff haffn't helped."

"Yes, I'm sorry about that."

"Oh, it's all right. It will foon heal up, if I keep gargling." He dipped under the water, then popped back up and threw back his head. "Gargalargalargle." Then he spat out the water. "Ah, that's better."

Now that Holly was close it was easy to see he wasn't really silver, but she wasn't disappointed.

"You know, I'm glad you're not silver, because if you were I'd never have met you."

"Wouldn't you?"

"No. Because you'd sink to the bottom, and anyway, if fish were silver there wouldn't be fish for very long."

"Oh, why?"

"Well, it would be a really easy way to get rich, if you could just fish for silver."

Holly had to explain to Silverfish what silver was, and how it was very valuable, and in the old days it was used as money. The fish seemed very interested. Not that you could tell by looking at him. Well, fish can't look interested. They can't look anything really, apart from fishy; but he didn't interrupt, so I think we can assume he was interested.

At the end of Holly's explanation Silverfish said, "Fo it'f really valuable thif filver ftuff if it?" He ducked under the water and gargled again before continuing. "And it shines like me and it doesn't float?" Holly nodded. "Oh, I see you've got a fishing rod."

"Yes," replied Holly, "but I don't want to fish any more. The thing about fishing is I enjoy the sandwiches and the little folding chairs and the big umbrellas, but it's a bit boring waiting for a bite and then when we finally got a bite I didn't really like it."

"So you let me go."

"Yes."

"But if you thought I was silver, I could have been worth a lot of money." Holly hadn't really thought about that until now.

"Well," she said, "I suppose some things are worth more than money."

"I don't think your father sees it like that."

"Yes, he'll be disappointed, but he's a fisherman, they're used to that. He'll still talk about you as though he'd caught you. You'll be the one that got away and you're quite a size."

"Charming – he's no small fry himself."

"He said you were a chub."

"He's really got it in for me, hasn't he?"

"No, it's a type of fish," Holly added hastily, thinking she was getting into deep water. "No offence meant."

"And none taken I'm sure. Well, I just wanted to say thank

you and show my gratitude."

"Oh, that really isn't ..." But he had already gone.

Holly was halfway back across the bridge when there was a splash below her. She looked down.

"Here, fling your hook!" It was Silverfish. But what did he want? "Come on, hurry up, before somebody comes – drop your line down here."

Holly swung her rod out over the water and released the line. She felt a tug as the hook was pulled down into the water. Then it stopped. "What now?" she thought. There was a pause, and then two sharp tugs on the line.

"It's a signal," she thought, and started to haul in the line, which wasn't easy without a proper reel. There was something on the hook now, and it was very heavy. Then she saw a flash of silver in the water.

"Oh no," she thought, "I've caught him again. I'd better haul him in and free him." The line got heavier as she slowly pulled it up. Finally it jumped from the water and she saw it wasn't Silverfish on the end of the line, but what looked like an old muddy tin jug.

"Thanks, Silverfish," she thought. "Just what I never wanted." There was a splash in the water and Silverfish flipped his way up river, flicking his tail fin in and out of the water. Holly waved back.

As she cleaned off the old tin jug Holly felt rather sad. She wondered if she'd ever see Silverfish again.

The story was on the front page of the local paper the following Tuesday: "Local girl finds thirteenth-century silver drinking vessel". There was a picture of Holly standing on the bridge with her "old tin jug". Now it was cleaned up you could see that the handles were in the shape of two silver fish. There was also an interview with an eminent archaeologist who pointed out that there had been a bridge at that point in the river since AD 905 and that somebody probably dropped the jug when they were leaning over the bridge trying to fill it.

And, of course, there was Holly's story, but who'd believe that? After all everybody knew that Holly was a chatterbox, and anyway it was probably just another fisherman's tale.